Her Christmas Cowboy

A Scott Brother Romance

KATHERINE GARBERA

TULE

Her Christmas Cowboy
Copyright © 2016 Katherine Garbera
Tule Publishing First Printing, October 2016

The Tule Publishing Group, LLC

ALL RIGHTS RESERVED

No part of this book may be used or reproduced in any manner whatsoever without written permission except in the case of brief quotations embodied in critical articles and reviews.

This is a work of fiction. Names, characters, places, and incidents are products of the author's imagination or are used fictitiously. Any resemblance to actual events, locales, organizations, or persons, living or dead, is entirely coincidental.

ISBN: 978-1-945879-57-9

Her Christmas Cowboy

WELCOME TO THE TOWN OF MARIETTA, WHERE MANY MONTANA BORN LOVE STORIES COME TO LIFE.

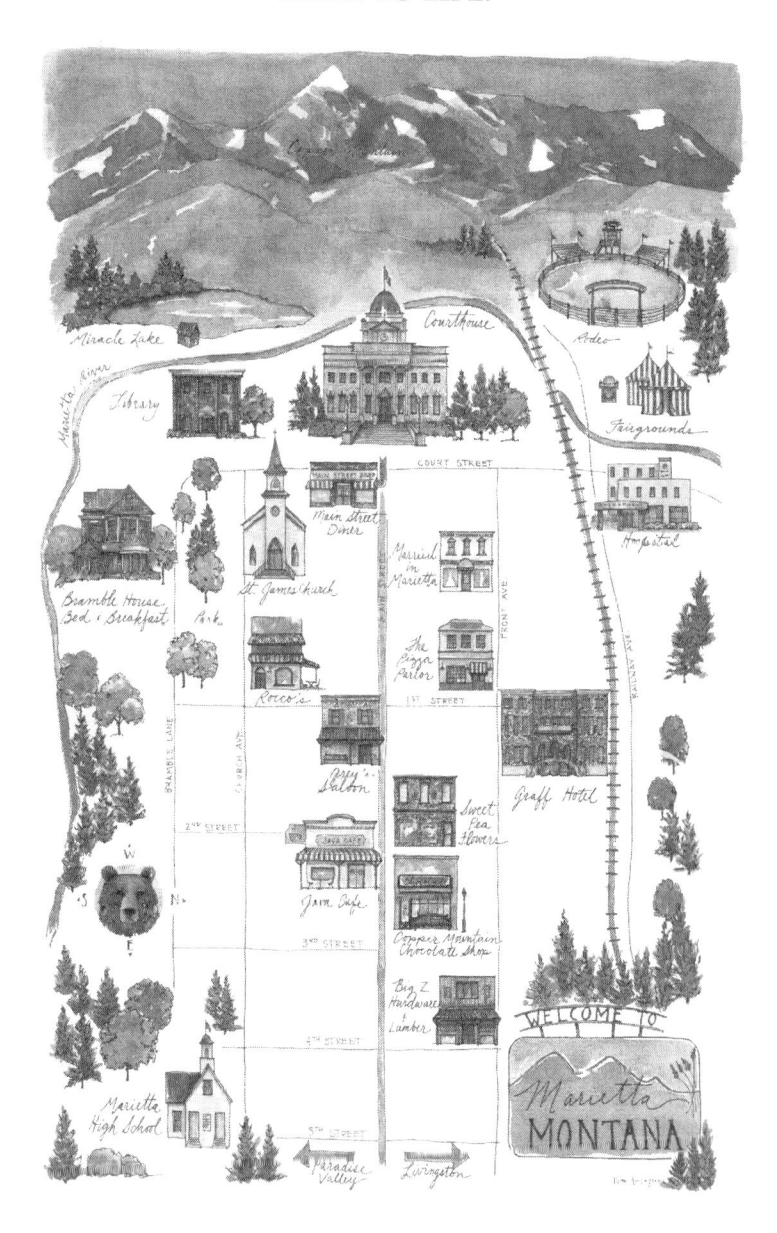

Chapter One

Christmas decorations hung from all of the lampposts on Main Street and as she walked slowly up toward the loft apartment she rented over Sweet Pea Flowers, Felicity Danvers tried to make herself feel something. There was a crisp breeze and it felt almost as if she were in a Currier and Ives print. But the magic of Christmas just wasn't here…not this year.

Christmas had once been the highlight of her year but now she struggled to muster much more than…well exhaustion. She was busy at the elementary school celebrating all of the seasonal events with her students. And her mom kept texting her about parties that Felicity and her sister were expected to attend. There was a holiday tea with her extended family, that which was going to be held at the Graff Hotel, a Christmas Ball at the Graff, a tree-decorating party at her sister's, a cookie party that she had to bake three dozen cookies for and of course the Marietta Stroll, the nativity play, and then shopping.

She stumbled on a patch of ice.

She felt her feet flying out from under her as she started

to fall. Someone grabbed her arm and they both wobbled and then fell over. She found herself staring up into a pair of eyes that were dark as night.

She knew those eyes. Enigmatic, dark blue with a hint of gray around the irises. There were sun lines around the corners of his eyes and thick, straight brown hair that fell over his eyes.

Lane Scott.

"I'm sorry," she said, embarrassed that she might have caused the decorated retired Marine to fall. They'd been in the same high school class and she had no excuses for avoiding him since he'd returned to Marietta three years ago. Except he was a double amputee and every time she'd thought about talking to him she hadn't been able to think of a single thing to say. Should she mention the injuries? Continue to ignore them?

"Don't be. This is the best fall I've had lately," he said, putting his arms around her and shifting them both to a seated position.

His strength surprised her. His arms bulged as he lifted her and moved her around.

"You're really strong," she said, then mentally smacked herself. This was precisely why she'd avoided Lane. She sounded pitiful.

Giving her a sardonic look from under his eyelashes, he said, "Thanks."

"I'm an idiot," she said.

"No, you're not. Give me a second and I'll help you up."

She glanced over and noticed he was adjusting his left leg and then his right. Once he had his feet on the ground, he stood up and offered her his hand.

She moved around until she could stand, took his hand, and stood up next to him. He was tall—well, he always had been probably a smidge under six foot. Glancing down at his feet she saw he had on a pair of western boots. He had probably been working out at the Scott Christmas Tree Farm. All of the Scott family pitched in to help at this time of year—even though Carson owned and ran the tree farm.

"What were you thinking about?" he asked. "You were distracted."

"Just going over all the things I need to do before December 25th. I'm sorry I fell into you."

"It's not the first time." He grinned. "Want to grab some hot chocolate at Sage's?"

Did she? She had just been saying how she had no time, but there was something about Lane Scott that had always gotten to her. The fact that he had asked her out in high school and she'd said no, the fact that he was a hero and she was afraid to talk to him. The fact that...heck, she just wanted to say yes.

Why shouldn't she?

"Sure. But it's my treat."

"Done," he said.

They walked in a sort of amiable silence...well, she

thought it might be amiable on his part, but she was trying to find something to say. Her problem was that she was curious about his prosthetic limbs and his life with them. She wanted to ask him about it but didn't know the polite way to do it.

So instead she was stuck with mundane things to talk about. Christmas. She could talk about the holiday.

"Are you going to the Christmas gala at the Graff?"

He groaned. "It's not that I want to, but if I don't I'm afraid my brothers will gang up on me. I have been staying out of town to avoid that kind of thing, but since it's Christmas…"

"I know exactly what you mean. I really thought about heading somewhere tropical and not returning until January 10th."

"Why the 10th?" Lane asked.

"Then I'd avoid the aftermath of Christmas. Mom always schedules a brunch to do a Christmas postmortem."

Lane laughed. "Your mom sounds…"

"Crazy," Felicity said. "Just kidding. She loves Christmas so much and wants us to have the best holiday every year. But the pressure is too much, you know?"

"I actually don't know. Mom's been gone for almost fifteen years now and Dad never made much of an effort. Lately, my nephews have been the focus of the holidays but really that's homier than a lot of functions. We work, we sled and snowshoe, and then we string popcorn and sing songs.

But that's about it."

"That sounds perfect," she said, glancing over his shoulder and noticing her mom barreling down Main with a determined look on her face.

Felicity groaned and grabbed Lane's shoulders, turning him to block her from view. "Sorry about this but my mom is across the street and it looks like she is on the warpath."

"Warpath?"

"Someone probably doesn't have enough Christmas decorations in their front room," Felicity said. "I think I might have to take a rain check on Sage's."

"How about a drive out of the city? They serve Sage's hot chocolate at the tree farm," Lane said.

She looked up at him—those blue-gray eyes of his so sincere—and she knew that she should say no. She had broken up with her boyfriend six months earlier and she'd realized that she liked being on her own. Everyone in town said Lane needed a woman. He needed someone who would be good for him and settle him down. Welcome him back to Marietta for good.

Felicity wanted to stay clear so that one of those marriage-minded Marietta woman could do just that for Lane. But she also really wanted to get out of town and she liked him.

"Okay."

★

LANE HADN'T MEANT to ask her out. In fact, given his mood he should have said good-bye and headed toward Grey's Saloon, but *should have* had never really been his strong suit. So instead he found himself sitting in the cab of his truck, heading toward the tree farm that was owned and run by his brother Carson.

He knew it wasn't very nice but he was a little sick of his brothers and their well-situated lives. He wasn't sure if he wanted what they had or not. All he knew was if he had to spend one more meal listening to stories of their domestic bliss he was going to lose it.

His brothers used to be rowdy hell-raisers who spent most of their time teasing and tormenting each other. Now they were talking about PTA events, whether his nephews were too old to believe in Santa, and what they were going to do if Emma had a girl—she and Hudson didn't know the sex of the baby she was expecting but all of the Scotts had decided they'd have to gang up on the boys in town to keep their niece safe.

Damn him. He loved it. He loved that his brothers had found women to make their lives easier, but he also just wanted…to want something. He had been in limbo for a long time. It hadn't helped that Marcy had broken up with him just as he'd been recovering from the explosion—to be fair she'd sent the email before he'd stepped on the IED. He just hadn't received and read it before he'd been injured. And then recovering had taken all his energy.

Now he was back home and desperately ready to be normal—except he couldn't connect to anyone. He was faking everything and not sure he would ever really feel anything again.

Until she'd run him down. Felicity had made him laugh and smile. So that was why he was here and not over at Grey's.

"Do you already have a tree?" he asked. There was an aura of melancholy around her.

"I don't. I have been debating buying a fake tree—don't tell anyone," Felicity said.

"The outrage," Lane said. "Carson has some that are in large clay pots, so you can have the tree delivered every year if you are worried about cutting down a tree and then throwing it out."

"Not really." Felicity blushed. "I mean of course I don't want to be wasteful."

He had to smile. Felicity Danvers was exactly how he remembered her from high school. Sweet and shy and sometimes blunt almost to the point of being inappropriate.

"It's okay. Why were you thinking fake tree?"

She made a face. "Just for the ease of it. I could pull it out of the box and decorate it… I mean I could even leave the lights on it from year to year."

"That would be nice," he said.

"Do you do that?"

"No. I put the lights on my tree every year. But I do get

one in a clay pot…actually it's one I planted when I was a boy," Lane said. His mom had started the nursery and tree farm that Carson ran now. They provided cut trees and potted ones for many of the families in Marietta and in neighboring ranch areas.

"That's so sweet. We have a Christmas quilt that we've been making since I was a girl. Andrea, my mom, and I each make a square every year and add it to the quilt. My mom started hers the year she and Dad got married so it's pretty big now. Mine's not quite big enough to cover the bed."

"I love that tradition," Lane said.

"Thanks. And thanks for helping me get out of town. It's just been a long day. I'm usually not this wimpy."

"I didn't think you were wimpy," he said. "Want to talk about it?"

Something about him seemed to make everyone want to talk to him. He didn't know whether it was simply because most people knew a lot of crap about him due to his injuries and they wanted to level the playing field, or if it was because of "his baby face" as Hudson liked to say.

"Nothing worth talking about. Just ran into my ex and he always makes me feel icky."

"Sorry about that," Lane said. "Exes can be that way."

"They can be, which is why they are exes. I guess I'll see about getting one of those clay pot trees," Felicity said as they turned off the main highway and found a parking space outside the Scott Christmas tree lot.

Carson had the lot set up with a tent that served Sage's famous hot chocolate and gingerbread and other holiday goodies. There were horse-drawn sleigh rides for families and of course the opportunity to select and cut down the Christmas tree of choice.

"This is nice. Thank you again."

"You're very welcome," he said. He took her to get hot chocolate and realized that people were staring at them.

"Guess you don't date much," Lane said.

Felicity groaned. "It's not that. They're probably thinking you deserve someone better than me. I broke up with my ex very publicly by throwing a drink on him and have been lying low since then. Sorry, Lane—gosh I say that a lot around you. But it's sincere."

"It's all right. So I'm the first guy you've been seen with since the breakup?"

"Yup. Sorry about that."

"Nothing to be sorry about; we're friends, right?"

She looked up at him, her eyes bright and hopeful with just a hint of the lingering sadness. "We are friends."

"Good," he said. "Do you need help picking out your tree?"

She shook her head. "Besides I see Carson waving furiously at you. I think you're needed."

"Not if you need me," Lane said.

"That's very sweet but honestly I'm good for now. I'll get one of the hands to take me back to town as well. Thanks for the ride."

Lane wanted to argue but he felt like she was trying to get away and he let her go. Besides lifting and carrying a Christmas tree into her house wasn't something he could do. As he watched her go, he realized that he wanted to be able to do that.

Was that what this ennui was about? The fact that being home made it harder to feel normal, since he remembered the man he used to be and there wasn't a bridge between the past and the present for him?

Well this Christmas he was determined to figure it out and make the next year one where he felt alive again.

Chapter Two

THE STROLL.

She knew that she had no reason to avoid it. In a way she was looking forward to seeing Lane. She'd flaked out the last time because she'd felt like she'd been in a fishbowl, but the truth was she liked Lane. She still had the feeling of…excitement in the pit of her stomach when she thought of him.

The Stroll was just getting into full swing and a light snow had begun to fall. She carefully rewrapped her scarf around her neck and pulled her beanie more snugly down around her ears.

It was cold. She couldn't help wishing she were somewhere warmer. Like maybe in her loft apartment acting like a recluse.

"Miss Danvers! Miss Danvers!"

She glanced around and saw Evan Scott running toward her. He'd been in her second grade class three years ago. And had grown a lot since then. He was taller and he smiled more easily. Felicity knew that getting a new mom had helped him a lot.

His thick brown hair fell over his forehead and someone had made a valiant effort at taming his cowlick. He had bright eyes that reminded her of Lane's. Only fair given that Evan was his nephew. He had those distinctive thick Scott eyebrows and was already starting to swagger a little when he walked. In a few years he'd be following in his father's and uncles' footsteps and causing Marietta girls to stare when he walked by.

But right now he still had that boyish innocence that made her smile.

"Evan, how are you?"

"I'm good. This year I get to help with the sleigh rides." He blushed a little as he looked up at her.

"What are you doing?"

"Driving the team," Evan said.

"I get to help too," his cousin, JT, said. "Of course Uncle Carson and Uncle Lane are helping us. But next year it will be just us."

It was hard to believe these little guys were growing up so quickly. That was her problem this year. Everyone else seemed to be moving forward and she was still dodging her mom, volunteering at the senior center, and spending most nights alone. She needed a change but had been so afraid to make one.

"Well, I will definitely be by later to have a sleigh ride with one of you two."

"Yay! See you then," Evan said, giving her a cheeky grin

that reminded her of Lane before dashing off through the light crowds toward the park.

Felicity stepped out of the stream of people walking on Main Street and leaned against the wall of the Main Street Diner.

She watched the crowds and tried to deal with the revelation she'd had while watching those two little kiddos that she'd known since they were born. Seeing their lives changing…while hers stayed still.

"Penny for your thoughts."

She glanced around; saw Lane standing not two feet from her. "That's not a good deal. My thoughts aren't worth much right now."

Lane reached for her arm, squeezed it, and looked down at her with such concern that it her melted a little. It didn't matter that this was Lane Scott—the boy who'd always been destined for great things—and she was little old Felicity who was destined for hometown anonymity. He cared.

She forced a smile. "Yeah, just feeling sorry for myself."

"Want to talk about it? I'm told I'm a very good listener."

"Nah," she said. She didn't want to say anything that would make her seem more pitiful in his eyes. So far every time she'd seen him she'd been in the middle of dodging the holiday: the first time she'd been running from her mom, and now she was feeling sorry for herself. She wanted to impress him, so instead she kept showing him…well who she really was.

"What was it like to be away from here for Christmas?" she asked.

He tipped his head to the side. Cupping his hand under her elbow, he started walking, bringing her with him. "It was different. I was in the desert so there was no snow, no real greenery. My unit had a tree we'd rigged up in our barracks, but it was made from leftover paper towel rolls. I was happy with the job I was doing so I felt at home there. The second Christmas, I was homesick. I think about that sometimes—how the first year I was so excited to be serving my country, protecting everyone back home. Nothing really bothered me then."

"What happened in the second year?" she asked.

"That's a story for another time. Maybe over dinner?"

She pursed her lips and tried to think of a nice way to decline. Nothing had changed. She still liked Lane a little more than she should, and saying yes had the potential to bring out her overly chatty side.

Plus, a part of her couldn't help thinking that Lane deserved a woman like Kylie. She was single and sweet and also taught second grade. Everyone praised her…well everything. Even her mom had one time said she should try to be more like Kylie.

"I'm not—"

"Is it because of my handicap?" he asked. "It's okay if that's the reason, but I'd prefer to know so I can stop asking you out."

She flushed. This was precisely what she'd been worried about. She'd screwed up even trying to protect him. "No. That's not it."

They were almost to the park and she took his wrist in her hand and drew him off the footpath. She was embarrassed that he thought that. And ashamed. Her fears and doubts had driven her decisions. She didn't want him to think that he was anything other than…well, perfect in her eyes.

"It's me. I always had a crush on you. I'm not sure if I could act normal if we went to dinner or had drinks together. I think I'd be awkward and right now you seem to like me; I don't want to ruin it."

He shook his head. "You have the oddest way of showing things. I asked you out twice in high school…"

"I know," she said. Another thing she'd have to regret. "You were so cute and I was afraid to talk to you. So I just said no. It was the one word I could say around you."

"I was cute?"

"Yeah, you still are, Lane. Don't let it go to your head," she said.

He stood a little taller and gave her a wink. "Don't worry, I won't. I'm picking you up tomorrow afternoon at three. Dress warmly."

"Where are we going?"

"On our first date," Lane said with another wink and a

tip of his Stetson before he walked away.

She watched him go, realizing he had a nice butt and a very nice swagger.

★

"Caught ya," Hudson said walking up behind Lane. His older brother slung an arm around Lane's shoulders as they both walked toward the sleigh ride area that had been set up on the far side of the park.

"Doing what?"

"Flirting with the cute elementary school teacher."

"So?"

"So nothing, just glad to see you acting like a Scott."

"How is flirting acting like a Scott?" he asked his brother. Ever since Hud had come home from the road and settled down with Emma, his brother was…well odd. He had spent a lot of hours at the Ka-Pow gym talking to Lane about the merits of falling in love and finding "the one". It would have been funny if Lane hadn't sort of wanted to find what Hud had. He couldn't. He knew that.

Mostly because he'd had real trouble engaging emotionally and he spent a lot of time on the road. Talking about what had happened to him to other injured servicemen had been important to him in the beginning, and he liked the honest exchange he always shared when he was with them.

It took a lot of effort to keep up the illusion that he was normal. That he'd licked his wounded veteran status and moved on. The truth was most days he knew he was lucky to be alive and he was grateful for all that he had, but he still felt…angry, resentful. Unsure of the future.

"We do it better than other men," Hud said.

"What do you do better?" Emma Jean said as she came up to Hudson, slipping her arm around his waist and tipping her head back.

"Flirt, Emma—he thinks he flirts better," Lane said, with a grin at his pregnant sister-in-law.

"Well he is pretty good at that, but I can think of a few things he's better at," Emma said.

"Yeah, darlin', like what?"

"Being stubborn," she said, tipping her head to the side. "I thought I told you to wear that scarf tonight. You were coughing this morning." Emma's tone was scolding but also caring.

"I don't need a scarf," Hud said, drawing Emma away. Lane walked on, leaving his brother and sister-in-law behind as the conversation turned quiet and intimate.

He felt that pang in his gut as he approached the sleigh ride kickoff area and noticed Carson and Annie talking quietly together. Everyone was coupled up and he was…not. He could find a gal for himself; he knew that. There'd been no shortage of offers since he'd come back to Marietta, and to be honest in the other cities he'd visited he didn't do too bad either.

But there was no one special. It was hard to tell if a

woman was interested in him for himself or because they felt sorry for him. Not a nice thing to think; he knew it. But then again sometimes he wasn't a nice man. Though the townsfolk in Marietta were used to him being back, they still treated him like he was so brave and he'd heard the word "hero" more than once—mostly when he'd first come home. But he wasn't a hero.

He'd been a guy doing a job and his entire life had changed because of it. That didn't make him a hero. Even after his injury when he'd started turning to athletics, skiing and running with the special prosthetics that had been made for him, he didn't see that as something praiseworthy. He needed to exercise. Needed to stay busy and keep moving. Couldn't stay still.

Even now.

Even with Felicity to flirt with and to distract him, he was afraid to take a deep breath and to say he was home. Home had changed when he'd been on a medical transport being shipped back to the States, hoping that the damage to his legs wasn't as bad as it had turned out to be.

The idea of home was gone. Even now that he was back in Marietta using it as a base to go on his speaking engagements and all of his brothers were back. Hud had made his peace with Dad and there was no reason for Lane to still have this gnawing emptiness inside of him, but it remained.

Had remained for too long.

Felicity couldn't change that.

"Uncle Lane?"

He glanced down to see Evan at his elbow. That little guy had had a growth spurt at the beginning of the school year and was getting taller by the day. "Yeah, kiddo?"

"Dad said I'm supposed to work with you on Sleigh One. I've been practicing a lot and I hoped you'd let me take the reins when Miss Danvers comes for a ride."

Felicity again.

"Sure will. You can practice all night. I remember the first time I was at the reins," Lane said. It seemed so long ago; he'd been just about Evan's age. His mom had been the one to ride with him.

"Did you have any accidents? JT said that his dad ran the sleigh up onto the sidewalk."

"Alec was busy looking at Aunt Sienna when he did that," Lane said.

"How'd that make him mess up?" Evan asked.

"Girls can distract a guy," Lane said. He led Evan to the team that they'd be using today, and together they checked the reins and the blinders on the horses. It was important that the horse wasn't spooked and blinders were the best way to ensure that.

"I won't get distracted," Evan said. At ten, Lane was pretty sure that his nephew wouldn't get distracted. But in a few years he might not find it so easy to keep his concentration.

"Why do you want to drive for Miss Danvers?" Lane

asked.

"She's really nice and pretty."

"Make sure you keep your eyes on the horses and not on Miss Danvers," Lane said.

Maybe Evan would need his help this year. It seemed Felicity had cast her spell—not just on Lane but also on Evan.

He got Evan up in the driver's seat of the sled and turned to greet his first customers. Lane knew this was going to be a long afternoon and evening. Everyone in town knew him and knew his story. He kept his smile in place and tipped his hat to all the ladies and answered the questions they had for him.

People in town always made him feel that they were so happy he was back and that he was healthy. And Lane knew they meant well, but with each new well-wisher he felt his skin tighten.

He felt like he needed to get off of Main Street and maybe out of Marietta—but he couldn't. He had promised his dad he'd stay home. Promised his brothers he was back to normal. The old Lane.

He hadn't realized what a huge lie that was until this moment.

★

WAYLAID BY HER Mom, Felicity had spent most of the afternoon and evening at the Marietta Paws booth taking holiday photos of kids and their pets. It was fun and kind of quelled the unsettled feeling she had inside. But as Nat King Cole sang "The Christmas Song" and families and their pets donned Santa hats, she was distracted.

Lane.

His no-nonsense invitation lingered in the back of her mind. She felt a little tingle in the bottom of her stomach and wanted to pretend it was the thrill of Christmas and the beginning of the season that was finally catching up with her, but she couldn't lie to herself.

She knew better than to pretend that Christmas could hold a candle to Lane Scott. She'd been crushing on him for the longest time. In high school of course, but really it had happened when he'd come back to Marietta. When he'd returned and shown her that any setback she'd experienced in her life shouldn't keep her from moving forward.

Frank Sinatra was crooning about being home for Christmas when Risa came and relieved her at the photo booth.

"Time's up," Risa said.

Risa was the town florist and Felicity's landlord. "Thanks."

"Monty and I are having a tree-decorating party next Thursday. Drop-in between six and eight. We'd love to see you there," Risa said.

Felicity nodded. "I'd love to come. Is it potluck?"

"Desserts only. Monty said he'd rather have leftover

cookies and cakes than leftover casserole. It's a good thing he spends most of his time at the gym with his sweet tooth."

Felicity smiled at Risa. Monty had nothing to worry about. The retired Marine was fit and still worked for a special operations group. She'd seen him working out with Hudson and Lane at Ka-Pow when she arrived early for her kickboxing class.

Actually if she had to admit it, the first time she really noticed Lane was when she'd seen him and Monty sparring with each other. They used mixed martial arts and Lane was never at a disadvantage. He'd fought like a man who knew what he was doing, and every time they'd finished even or he'd bested Monty.

She caught her breath, thinking about how his muscles had glistened with sweat. Okay so maybe she had spent too much time watching him work out and not enough paying attention to her own kickboxing lesson, but it was Lane.

"Great. We look forward to seeing you then," Risa said, waving her off.

Felicity walked away, her mind not on the tree-decorating party at all. But instead on Lane. With that thought in mind, she drifted over to the sleigh ride line, which was pretty long. She sort of wanted to bug out and go home but she'd promised Evan and JT, and she didn't want to break her word.

Her mom had always said that kids needed to know that adults were solid. That once they said they'd do something good or bad they needed to follow through.

"Sweetie, there you are. How are you enjoying the Stroll?"

Her mom gave her a one-armed hug and handed her a thermal mug that smelled like Sage's hot chocolate. "I'm enjoying it. The pet booth was a fun place to volunteer. Want to join me on a sleigh ride?"

"I'd love to, sweetie, but I promised Myrtle that I'd bring her something hot to drink—and since I just gave you her drink, I'm going to have to go and get her another one."

"I haven't drunk out of this one—"

"It's okay, you look cold. Take it with you on the sleigh ride. Are we still on for breakfast in the morning?" her mom asked.

"Yes. But I have a date at three, so I can't stay too long," Felicity said.

"A date? With whom?"

"Lane," she said.

Her mom nodded. "I heard you two were together the other day… Is this serious?"

"I don't know," she said. "Right now we're just old friends hanging out."

"That's the best place to start," her mom said. "Maybe see if he has a date for the Christmas Ball."

She groaned. "No, Mom. I'm not going to do that. We're friends and this is just a first date. He might not even like me."

"Honey, everyone likes you," her mom said, kissing her on the cheek and then waving good-bye as she went off to get Myrtle's hot chocolate.

Her mom meant well. Felicity knew that. After her father had died after Felicity's senior year of high school, her mom had spent six months in a very deep depression before she'd started volunteering. Since then her mom had been a whirlwind. Always going and doing.

Sometimes Felicity thought that was when she'd lost herself. First with Dad and then with trying to coax Mom back out of the house. She'd had a scholarship to go to school in California at UCLA but had deferred and then transferred to MSU in Bozeman. It had been so long since she'd done something just for herself.

"Miss Danvers, you came!" Evan said as she stepped up for her turn.

"I said I would," she said. "Wouldn't want to miss being driven by my favorite cowboy."

Evan blushed and smiled at her.

"Let me help you into the sled," Lane said, coming up to her. He held his hand out and she took it. He leaned in as she stepped toward the running board on the sled.

"I was hoping to be your favorite cowboy," he said with a wink. "Guess I'm going to have to work hard to change your mind."

She didn't have a chance to respond since he stepped back. But as she settled into the seat and Lane helped her get the blanket over her lap, she knew she had more than one favorite Scott cowboy.

Chapter Three

LANE WOKE UP early on Sunday morning with an itch in his big toe. Phantom sensation was nothing new to him but it was unnerving every single time it happened. He threw the covers off his body and sat up, putting his weight on his elbows, looking down his body. His thighs were heavily muscled and if he were being honest, stronger than before his injury. Then he got to where his knees used to be and saw the ends of his legs.

No toes to itch. Just scarring that had healed over and his new reality. He maneuvered himself to the edge of the bed and got out. He walked on his stubs to the bathroom and, using the stool that was there, washed his face. He put his hands on the countertop and looked up, stared at his own blue eyes in the mirror.

As always, he wasn't sure what he wanted to see, but he continuously disappointed himself. His therapist at the VA had said that the physical changes were often matched by an internal manifestation of something. She couldn't tell him what that change would be since it was different for everyone. And Lane kept hoping that it would be something monumental. That when he looked in the mirror he'd see a man with an inner conviction, but instead, he just saw himself.

He turned away from the mirror, climbed down off the stool, and went downstairs to make himself some coffee.

He'd made some adjustments to his home after he'd purchased it and had a few of the countertops lowered so that he didn't always have to wear his prosthetics.

His brother Trey lived in the house next door in the development with his new wife Lucy. Trey was a photojournalist and still went on jobs that took him away from Montana, but he was spending more time at home now. Which explained the loaf of banana bread on his breakfast table. Lucy was a chef and owned a breakfast-only café. She had a spare key to his place and always left him little treats like this.

He rubbed his hand over his chest.

He liked this about Marietta.

He wanted Marietta to feel like home again.

But the emptiness inside of him kept growing and he was starting to realize it was something that wasn't going to just fix itself.

He levered himself onto a chair at the breakfast table after he'd put his coffee on the surface and pulled the banana bread loaf closer. Realizing he'd forgotten to get a knife, he cursed and tore a chunk of the loaf off.

Some mornings it was more effort than it was worth to

be normal. To just get up and walk on his stubs to the drawer and get the forgotten knife.

He cursed under his breath.

He was supposed to pick Felicity up for a date at three, but he was in a foul mood. He reached for his cell phone and texted Monty. His old Marine buddy was always there. Lane knew partially that was because Monty and he had flipped for which side of the street each of them would clear, and Lane had stepped on an IED right after that. Monty wasn't to blame for the injury but his best friend felt like he was.

Lane: *I need to work out. Gym?*

But before he hit send, he thought of Monty at home with his wife and realized that the last thing he wanted to do was disturb his friend. Monty deserved whatever peace he had with Risa and Lane wasn't about to interrupt that. Everyone had scars from the Middle East.

He turned his phone upside down on the table and sat there. Emotions roiling through him like a snowstorm blowing in over Copper Mountain. There wasn't a damned thing he could do to stop it. He just had to sit there and let the resentment and anger build in him.

His phone vibrated on the table and he cursed again, hoping he hadn't sent that text message to Monty by accident. He turned the phone over and saw it was from an unknown number.

He opened the message app on his phone.

UNKNOWN NUMBER: *Hey, it's Felicity. I am going to brunch at my mom's this morning and she said to invite you to join us. You can say no. I want to say no. She's probably going to recruit you to help set up the nativity in front of her house.*

Felicity.

Immediately an image of her last night when he'd tucked her into the sled popped into his head. Her long brown hair tucked under her hat, the tip of her nose a little red from the cold, the warmth from her touch as she'd held his hand.

Lane: *I'd love to. What time?*
Felicity: *Ten. We can meet at my place if you want.*
Lane: *I'll be there.*
Felicity: *:)*

He put his phone on the table and then got off his chair. He headed up the stairs feeling freer than he had before. His irritation at the day abated for now. He showered, put on his prosthetics that would accommodate his boots, and then got dressed in jeans and a flannel shirt.

As he walked downstairs he realized he was whistling "Jingle Bell Rock". He shook his head. He wasn't going to assign too much significance to the fact that Felicity had changed his mood. He went back into the kitchen, got a knife out of the cabinet, and cut off the jagged edge of the banana bread loaf in case Trey or Lucy stopped by later.

He didn't want them to see the results of his temper

from earlier. He washed up his coffee cup and then looked at the time. It was too early to go to Felicity's. But he didn't want to stay in the house. He took his keys from the hook by the door, donned his shearling coat, and stepped outside to see his brother shoveling his own walk.

Trey waved at him and Lane started to clear his own drive. He felt something shift and settle in him. He might not feel like he was home, but there were moments when everything was right in his world.

☆

FELICITY FOUND HERSELF standing in front of the small potted Douglas fir that she'd purchased three days ago at the Scott Tree Farm. The loft apartment that she called home was big and open. And her Christmas tree—while not in the Charlie Brown league—was dwarfed by the open space.

But she liked it.

It wasn't perfect and that made her smile. She'd resisted all of her mom's attempts to come and decorate her loft for her. She wanted to have some part of Christmas that wasn't perfectly planned, that was made up of simple things that made her happy.

She glanced at her watch one more time, but the seconds were going by slowly. She had that tingling in the pit of her stomach that felt like excitement. Lane was coming to her place.

Lane Scott.

She'd dreamt of him last night. They'd been in the sleigh that he and Evan had driven expertly on Main Street, but in her dream it had only been the two of them. They'd been snuggled together under the thick wool blanket and the sleigh had driven itself. Hey, it was a dream, things like that could happen.

But she'd woken this morning feeling restless. His face in her mind and the remembered feel of a kiss they'd never shared on her lips. She reached into one of the rubber tubs that housed her Christmas decorations and pulled out a shoebox with the year 2013 in glitter on it. She opened the box and smiled as she saw the ornaments her students had made for her that year.

Slowly she removed them and carefully hung them by their yarn fastenings on each of the branches. She worked her way through the shoeboxes until her tree was decorated with memories of former students. She had put on some white lights earlier and when she stepped back and flipped off the overhead lights so that only the tree was on, she felt a tingle of the holiday spirit.

Each ornament held a different memory. The sound of children's laughter seemed to echo in her mind as she searched for the angel she'd made herself when she'd been in elementary school.

Her mom had long ago relegated any handmade ornaments to the treasure box and not the tree. Felicity had taken it with her when she'd moved out. She figured that this toilet paper roll angel was the perfect topper for this tree.

She placed it on the top and then sank down on the rug in front of her tree. Just stared up at it and tried to keep that holiday feeling going, but it was fading. The more she thought of the treasure box and how only things that were perfect were allowed a place in her mom's holiday, the harder it was to stay happy.

Her mom never said anything to Felicity and there were times when she was almost positive that the attitude was coming from herself and not her mom, but she'd never felt like she was good enough for the front room tree.

She suspected that was why Johnny had broken up with her, the real reason why joy seemed always just a tiny bit out of reach. But it wasn't something she wanted to share. In fact, if she played her hand right no one else would ever have to know about her…well shame. It felt shameful no matter how she tried to twist it in her head.

Tears stung her eyes and she dashed them away.

She got to her feet, donned her boots, coat and hat, and went down the stairs. She'd wait for Lane outside. Where she wouldn't be alone with her thoughts. Maybe a walk down Main Street would clear her head.

As soon as she finished locking her door she heard the grumble of a pickup truck engine. She glanced toward the end of the alley to see a big, black Silverado pulling in. The truck rolled into the parking spot next to her Kia.

Lane got out of the truck, closed the door, and walked

around to lean against the fender. "I was afraid of being early but maybe I'm late."

He looked good. A light snow fell, dusting the top of his hat. He wore a tan-colored shearling jacket that was buttoned but left open at the collar so she could see his neck. He stood casually, but his hips were canted forward and she realized that he exuded confidence.

She wanted that.

Just a tiny taste of the confidence that he wore so well. And she knew she hadn't earned it, not the way Lane had. But she still coveted it.

"You're early. I just had to get out of my place."

"Why?" he asked.

They were friends…well, sort of. And the answer to that question wasn't something she would share with even her closest confidant, but a part of her wanted to tell him. "Sometimes my thoughts get to me."

He nodded. "Walking is a good cure for that," he said, coming over to her and holding out his hand.

She took it and he led her down the alleyway to the sidewalk of Main Street. There weren't many people out on a Sunday morning. In fact most people were either on the ranch doing chores or on their way to church. They walked in silence and it felt companionable.

Then she started to worry that maybe she should say something.

"Do you walk a lot?"

"Uh-huh. And shovel the walk in winter, or go over to Ka-Pow and work out. Moving almost always makes it easier to deal with whatever is going on in my head," he said.

She squeezed his hand. "I'm sorry you have to deal with that."

He stopped walking and looked down at her, his sky-colored eyes heavy with an emotion she couldn't read. "It was a choice I was very eager to make. I can't change my life."

"Would you want to?" she asked. His face was close. So close she could smell his minty breath and see the tiny green flecks in his irises.

"No. If I did I wouldn't be here now," he said, lowering his head toward hers.

She closed her eyes and went up on tiptoe.

☆

HER LIPS WERE soft and tasted of strawberries and summer. The temperature was bitterly cold, but it was December in Montana so that was a given. But the heat from her kiss warmed him. Energy tingled through his body, making him harden, and there was a tingle at the base of his spine that made him feel powerful and alive.

He put his hands on her shoulders because he wanted to grab her butt and pull her more fully into him. And his balance was sometimes iffy. The last thing he wanted was for them to fall and this kiss to end.

When he had her mouth under his, her tongue rubbing against his, he didn't feel that aching emptiness. He felt alive. Alive and powerful in a way that he hadn't in a long time. Sometimes he got close when he was skiing or running but never like this.

He tunneled his fingers under the band of her hat and into her hair. It was smooth and soft; he pushed the hat further up her head and off, tangling his fingers in the cool strands of her hair.

She tipped her head to the side, granting him greater access to her mouth, and he deepened the kiss. Took her mouth with surety. In this moment he wasn't faking it. In this moment he was normal. He was just a guy, kissing a girl who he'd wanted to kiss for too long.

He lifted his head, rubbed his lips back and forth against hers as he opened his eyes. Hers were closed and her lips were parted as he pulled back. He rubbed his thumb against her cheekbone and she opened her eyes. They were brown—not a deep dark chocolate color but more the colors of fall. Fall had always reminded him of home, maybe because when his mom had been alive that had been the season she'd loved the best.

But whatever the reason the warmth in his gut deepened. It wasn't just physical; though he wanted her with each breath he took there was another element. Something deeper and more profound.

Felicity.

"Kissing works too," she said, and then blushed. The pink color sweeping up from her neck and across her face. She dropped her gaze and he put his hand under her chin to lift her head back up until their eyes met.

"It does. Though that's not usually my way of distracting myself," he admitted. With Felicity he said the words that always seemed to burrow too deep. The ones he was afraid to admit to his brothers or Monty because they wouldn't know what to say back to him. But that didn't matter with her.

She tipped her head to the side. A strand of her hair fell forward over her face and he tucked it back behind her ear, noticing that she wore a pair of small gold hoops in her ears.

"Why not?" she asked.

"Kissing leads to complications," he said. "Surely, you've found that too."

Nibbling on her bottom lip, she turned from him and bent to retrieve her hat from the snowy sidewalk.

He groaned as the motion pulled her jeans tight against her hips and he couldn't help noticing she had a really fine ass. He reached out to touch her but dropped his hand before he made contact. He'd been trying to comfort her, not to seduce her, but this was Felicity. And since she'd run headlong into him four days ago, she'd been on his mind. Distracting him from the emptiness and the questions he wasn't sure he was ready to answer.

She noticed him staring at her backside as she stood and arched one eyebrow at him as she straightened. She put a hand on her hip.

"You've got a nice ass," he said. "Damn. I could have said that in a nicer way."

She shook her head, a grin teasing the corners of her mouth, and he realized this was the most relaxed and natural that he'd seen her.

"I liked it. You're too careful most of the time."

He was surprised she noticed since most people didn't.

"How do you know?"

"There's something...maybe a tone in your voice or a little look in your eye that gives you away," she said after a moment.

He didn't like that she saw him so clearly, but then he could see the desperation in her eyes too. He knew that she was running—but from what?

"Maybe we both see each other more clearly because we are both trying to hide in plain sight," he said. Taking her hand in his, he started to walk again. The park wasn't too far and he knew that if he kept moving he didn't feel as vulnerable as he would standing and looking into her eyes while they talked.

He was used to everyone thinking he'd put the injury and the war behind him. Used to everyone treating him like he was the greatest thing since sliced bread and to be honest he sort of needed it—or maybe he didn't. Maybe that was why he was feeling so out of sorts lately. Everyone treating him like he was okay when deep inside he knew he wasn't.

And here was Felicity treating him…like he was a guy she'd known in high school. Saying the right things and the awkward things, just being real with him.

And he knew that was what he needed. Felicity wasn't what he would have wished for this Christmas but only because he'd never have believed that a person could fill this emptiness. Not until this morning when he'd kissed her.

Chapter Four

A LOCAL MARIETTA craftswoman had made the nativity decades earlier. Lane could remember the first year it had shown up outside of the Danvers House. His mom had brought them all into town to buy their matching red flannel shirts for her holiday card picture and they'd ended up posing around the nativity.

The figures were clay that had been sculpted, fired, and then painted. As a boy Lane had stared into the face of Mary, trying to see a sign that she knew what was in store for her baby. He'd been going through a deeply religious phase at that time. It hadn't lasted long. The next year Missy Tobbin had let him kiss her under the mistletoe at school and girls had dominated his thoughts.

"These pieces are a lot heavier than I realized," Felicity said.

She'd gone a little bit into retreat mode after their kiss and he couldn't say he blamed her. Christmas was supposed to be fun and presents and family. Not sharing searing hot kisses in the snow…wait, why couldn't that be his Christmas?

Aside from the fact that he knew he wasn't ready to settle down. And Felicity was a hometown girl. Not like the gals he'd met on the road with the Invictus Games tour. She knew his family and if he messed with her, Lane was pretty sure he'd have to answer to his brothers and probably his nephews.

"They're not too bad," he said. "I'm on a heavy lifting schedule to get ready for a bike marathon I'm participating in next spring."

"You do a lot of events like that," she said. "I keep reading about your adventures in the *Marietta Gazette*. Do you think you'll ever settle back down here?"

He had thought he was settled but when she put it that way…

"I don't know," he said, honestly. "It's difficult sometimes because I'm not the man I was before I joined the Marines."

"I can see that," she said.

Was she referring to his legs? He told himself to let it go but he was in an odd mood today. Maybe he should have stayed home instead of coming to town and helping Felicity.

"Not just physically."

She gave him a startled look. "I didn't even think of that. You look the same physically to me. I meant in high school you were wild. Sort of like you had too much energy and didn't know where to direct it. And now, you seem very contained. Like you are in control of that wildness… Does that sound silly? I really don't mean it that way."

Once again she'd surprised him.

Which really shouldn't be shocking. Felicity seemed to see him with a clearer eye than most other people. He knew that there was a reason for it; he just didn't know what that reason was. Was it that she taught elementary school children? Kids had a way of seeing past the bullshit of everyday life and straight to the heart of what was really going on. And to be fair, Felicity did as well.

"It didn't sound silly," he said at last. "I think you are right. My mom had been sick in high school and I think I was acting out there—because I couldn't at home."

Felicity nodded. "I totally get that. My dad died the summer after high school. It changed everything. My plans, me…"

"I didn't know when he died," Lane said. "I'm sorry."

"Thanks. I'd like to say I'm used to him not being here, but you've lost a parent so you know it never goes away."

Lane nodded. She was so right. Most days he was okay with his mom being gone. Not okay exactly but he dealt with it. Then unexpectedly he'd get hit with a real sadness that she wasn't here. And it was never the same thing twice.

He couldn't explain it. But he didn't have to with Felicity. She just gave him that sort of half smile he was coming to love and went back to arranging the figures on her mom's front lawn.

The house looked like something that should be on

HGTV's Christmas decorating show. Mrs. Danvers took the holidays to the extreme. She was inside making her famous French toast casserole, which Lane had to admit he was looking forward to.

As soon as they had all of the figures arranged Felicity took his hand, surprising him as she tugged him backward. He lost his balance and started to fall, reaching out and careening into her.

She grunted as she took the full force of his weight and her surprised gaze met his. They slipped on the snowy ground and sort of awkwardly fell to the ground, ending up next to each other.

"Oh, God. I'm so sorry. I just forgot," she said. "I wanted to show you the best place to see the nativity."

He was angry again. Not at Felicity. Never at her. But at himself and at his fate. He didn't give into it often but today just felt like one of those days when he was having a hard time smiling and faking that he was okay.

He wasn't okay.

He hated that a girl he liked couldn't just grab his hand and pull him without him going over like a card house.

But this was his life.

She kept her eyes on him and he sensed she saw too much as always. He tried to fake a smile as hers faded and he knew that this wasn't going to work out the way he wanted it to. She knew he wasn't shaking this off.

"Lane—"

"Don't. Don't say anything else," he said and felt a little mean about the way he'd said it.

"Hey, what are you two doing?" Mrs. Danvers yelled from the porch. "Brunch will be ready in fifteen minutes."

"We're making snow angels," Felicity yelled back.

"You're too close together," her mom said.

"We don't mind if the angels aren't perfect, Mom," Felicity said.

Then she flopped onto her back next to him and he followed suit. She took his hand in hers and he glanced over to see that she was facing him. "No one has to be perfect."

★

FELICITY THOUGHT SHE'D ruined the morning but Lane's hand in hers, as they lay on their backs in the snow in her mom's front yard, was warm and comforting.

She moved her opposite arm and leg in a sweeping motion, knowing the snow angels they were making wouldn't be pristine, but this morning that didn't matter.

She was still a little upset that she'd forgotten about Lane's prosthetic legs. But she also thought that was probably a good thing. He was so…well, just Lane. Just a guy she knew from her hometown. For the moment she'd forgotten about all he'd been through, that he was a hero and should be treated with reverence and respect…not that she didn't respect him now, but it was nice to hang out with Lane and not worry about everything else.

He levered himself into a sitting position and pulled her up beside him. "I think we've made the sorriest-looking snow angels ever."

She nodded. "No doubt. Mom is probably going to come out here and make me rake over them so it doesn't mess up her lawn."

"Does she do that?"

"Let's just say that everything needs to look…well like a Currier and Ives print. She loves Christmas but really only when it resembles something out of a magazine, and sometimes I just want to make it more *Christmas Vacation*."

Felicity realized how that sounded and then wished she hadn't said anything. Her mom did the best she could. There were times when it was hard growing up with her. Even now her mom's demands for excellence made life hard for Felicity, but she knew her mom meant well. She just wanted everyone to have the perfect memory of the holidays.

It had been really hard after Felicity's dad had passed and her mom had been at a loose end that first year. Not unpacking a single decoration or ornament. But then she'd changed and started to make Christmas into the most beautiful and inspired holiday she could.

Her house was decorated better than the Graff Hotel. Her trees—and there was one in every room of the house—were all themed and perfectly balanced with lights and ornaments.

"I love it. It seems more elaborate than I remember from

when we were kids," Lane said, admiring the nativity.

"It is. She's gone decorating mad. She has a blog and a YouTube channel where she shows talks about Christmas year-round. It's actually kind of cute to watch her," Felicity said. "I think I sounded mean before and that wasn't fair."

"It's okay," Lane said. "My dad is difficult sometimes and I have four brothers to share the responsibility of taking care of him with. It's only you and your sister so that must be hard."

She nodded. "It is and it isn't. The three of us are pretty close and honestly, it's just this year that I'm struggling."

She didn't want to say why. Heck, she really didn't even want to think about it. The last year had been hard. Breaking up with her boyfriend. Starting another school year when she'd hoped that at some point she might leave Montana…then realizing she wasn't sure she wanted to anymore.

"With the holiday or something else?" he asked.

The question was too probing. Not that Lane could know that. But it wasn't one she wanted to answer honestly. Which made her mad at herself. Because lying or even fibbing about something like this wasn't what she wanted to do. But the truth was she was lost and talking about it wasn't something she thought would help.

"I guess the holiday," she said, at last. She stood up and held her hand down to him to help him to his feet.

He adjusted his legs, got his feet flat on the ground, and then reached up for her hand. And all the feeling-sorry-for-herself that she'd had going on disappeared. Lane was dealing with real problems—not like her. He had lost limbs and friends in Afghanistan and she had nothing to complain about when compared to him.

He took her hand and pulled himself up, and she wrapped her arms around him, hugged him tightly, and then stepped back. She was cold from lying in the snow and he was warm and solid. He represented things that she'd told herself she no longer wanted. But now she realized that had been one big fat lie.

"What was that for?"

"Me. I needed to hug you because I think you're brave, Lane Scott."

"I'm not really," he said. "Don't put me on a pedestal, Felicity. I'm just a guy who was doing a job he wasn't that fond of when he got injured. And everyone wants to thank me for it and I don't feel that I deserve anything."

She went up on tiptoe, putting her hands on his face and kissing him. Not the sweet gentle kiss of a friend but a tongue-tangling, soul-deep kiss that she hoped showed him how much he meant to her.

"You're so much more than you realize," she said, leading the way to the house before she said anything else. There were times when she really wished she had a better filter between her mouth and her brain. She didn't need to tell him all the ways she admired him, but the truth was she did admire him.

And she liked him.

And she wanted him.

And she wished…well, she wished he was hers. She looked over at the manger where the angel hung on top of the crèche looking down at the empty cradle where the baby Jesus would be placed on Christmas morning. It seemed as if the angel understood her wish.

But those sorts of wishes were…well, not real. She wasn't looking to settle down. She was just looking to get through the holidays. And this year it looked like lusting after Lane was how she was going to cope with it.

★

Mrs. Danvers had put on a good spread and Felicity was different around her mother. More reserved, more…well, proper for lack of a better word. When they were done eating they left after helping clean up the house. The walk back to Felicity's place was slow. Lane had plans for cross-country skiing out on his family's ranch but he didn't know if Felicity would enjoy it.

"The Mercantile always has the prettiest decorations for Christmas," Felicity said.

They'd gotten a little too close during those moments in her mom's front yard and now they'd both retreated behind their walls. He knew why he had them. Knew why he tried to keep a distance between himself and everyone else. But what was going on with Felicity?

She seemed like every other woman in Marietta to him. Smart, feisty, not really needing anyone, but there were moments when he saw the cracks in that façade. Moments when he caught a glimpse of some inner vulnerability that he just didn't understand.

And since he wasn't too sure what the future held for him, he sort of thought maybe he should just ignore it.

But he couldn't.

"What is the deal with you and your mom?" he asked. Completely ignoring her comment about the Mercantile. Who cared how they decorated? He really didn't think that Felicity wanted to talk about that anyway.

"None of your business," she said.

"I think it is."

"Why because we kissed each other?" she asked.

"Yes," he said. "And because we are friends."

Friends. He wanted them to be way more than that.

She leaned in, looking at him with that steady gaze of hers.

"I'm not really sure what's going on between us," she said. "Things with my mom are complicated and talking about it…well that's not for someone who's a casual friend."

There was nothing casual about the way he felt for Felicity and he couldn't help wondering if this was her running away again. She seemed to do that when things got too hot.

"I don't think of you that way."

She arched one eyebrow and then nodded. "Really?

You're going away again and I'm staying here."

He scrubbed a hand over the light stubble that he hadn't bothered to shave that morning and looked into her pretty brown eyes. She was serious. "Why do you think I'm leaving?"

She stopped walking, crossing her arms over her chest. "I think you have a calling and it's bigger than Marietta. What you experienced and how you've changed your life since being injured is inspiring. I know that you go to VA care centers and schools and talk, and you can't stop doing that."

"You're making assumptions about me," Lane said. The truth was he had no idea what his future held. He knew he wasn't back to normal like his brothers all assumed he was, but Marietta did call to him. He missed the mountains and the ranch. Working out at Ka-Pow and just being himself.

When he toured and talked everyone had an expectation of what he would say. And he was as honest as he could be, but the truth was there were times when it was…well a burden. But he hadn't figured out any other way to live his life.

The truth hit him hard as he watched Felicity. He had been stuck in limbo waiting for something…maybe it was her. Maybe it was just distance from his injury; he couldn't say. But this morning he felt different.

Like it was time to start making some different choices. Maybe he'd paid back the people who'd saved him and helped him move forward with his life after his injury. For just a little while, maybe it would be okay to take a break from being the wounded hero and just be Lane Scott.

Hell, he wasn't even sure he knew who Lane Scott was anymore.

But one thing was for certain: he wanted to get to know Felicity better. He didn't want her to look at him and see barriers or reasons why she couldn't trust him.

"I'm settled here," he said at last. "I came back home last year and I'm starting to really make my life here."

She nodded. "My mistake."

"Yes it was. Does it change things for you?" he asked.

She nodded.

"I want to keep seeing you," he said. "No use pretending that kiss this morning was enough for me."

She chewed her lower lip and tipped her head to the side as she studied him. "It wasn't enough for me either, but I'm not…"

She trailed off and he let her. He didn't push, even though he knew she was hiding something. There was more to his high school friend than he could guess. "Fair enough. I planned for a little cross-country skiing this afternoon. You up for it?"

"Yes. I'd like that. I put a pot roast in the slow cooker this morning, so if you'd like to, we can have dinner at my place after we ski."

"I'd like that," he said. "But sometimes my legs are sore after a full day. I might have to go back to my place for a soak in the tub."

There was no use pretending that he didn't have physical limitations. The fall earlier had already shown her the reality of his life. "I don't mind that at all. In fact, I have a really big claw-foot tub in the loft that you are welcome to use."

They joined hands again as they walked up Main Street and around to where his truck was parked. Lane refused to pretend he wasn't nervous. There was something about Felicity that made him ache, but not in the way he had been since he'd first come back to Marietta.

This wasn't that gnawing emptiness inside of him. This was a craving for something he'd thought he wouldn't feel again. This was the need to have someone special to share his life with. He was afraid he was projecting onto Felicity what he felt, but as they skied over land that had been in his family for generations, he felt like he wasn't fooling himself.

They had hot chocolate spiked with Frangelico with his brother Alec and his wife Sienna before heading back to town. Lane didn't realize until he pulled to a stop back behind Felicity's loft that for once he felt normal. He wasn't pretending everything was okay—for once it truly was.

Chapter Five

THE SNOW HAD started falling again as Lane parked his truck back at her loft apartment. The afternoon had been…well just what she needed. She hadn't felt the yoke of having to be perfect. Lane just accepted her at face value, which she appreciated.

Lane had taken her cross-country skiing on the Scott Ranch and they'd spent some time alone, skiing and talking. She hadn't realized how much tension she'd been carrying until she'd been alone with Lane.

"I know you said you sometimes ached after a long day… Do you feel like you could come up?" she asked. "Alec said you don't usually ski every weekend."

"Alec was trying to needle me," Lane said. "Like a pain in the ass big brother. I ski downhill most of the time and have competed in some exhibition X-Games type events for wounded vets."

"Sisters are different," Felicity said. "Andrea would wait until we were alone before teasing me about you. Do you want to come in?"

Lane grimaced a little. "Yes, I'd love to. I borrowed some

clothes from Alec, so if that offer to use your tub still stands…"

He trailed off. Something that wasn't like him, so she wondered if she'd made him uncomfortable by bringing up the fact that he might need to recuperate after the afternoon out.

"Would it be better if I never mentioned it? Your injury? I'm really not sure what to say or not to say, and I figured hedging around the truth wasn't going to make either of us comfortable."

He shook his head. "That would be foolish if I said pretend it's not a problem. No matter how normal I look on the outside, I'm still flawed."

She put her hand on his thigh and squeezed it. She didn't want Lane to feel that way. When she looked at him she saw so much more than most people had to endure and he made it look easy. She doubted it was, but he always seemed to just roll with it. It humbled her.

"Don't. Don't do that, Lane. You're not any more flawed than I am. We just all have different things that have damaged us."

"I don't know, Felicity; you don't seem too damaged to me," he said.

She shivered a little as the heat of the cab was evaporating. "Let's continue this discussion inside, unless you're going home."

He gave her a long, hard look out from under those thick

eyelashes of his and she could only stare at him. His face was becoming so dear to her. She knew the sun lines around his eyes, like the stubble on his jaw, and had studied too many times the scar in his left eyebrow. What was it from? Not that any of that mattered at this moment.

She realized she was holding her breath, waiting for his response, and let it out in a gush.

"I'm coming in. You promised me dinner," he said.

"That I did."

He took his seat belt off and leaned closer to her. Her breath caught again and her lips felt dry. She licked them and tilted her head closer to Lane's, but he reached past her—behind the seat—and pulled a duffel bag up and into his lap. She felt silly.

Like a silly girl who wanted a kiss from a cute boy. And the two parts of her that shaped who she was warred. The girl who'd been afraid of him in high school and the ballsy twenty-something who'd made some dumb choices because of cute boys and paid for them. But in the end this was Lane and she didn't want to let him go a second time.

She had been the one to say they should take it slow, but she knew she didn't want to. She wanted Lane Scott. She'd wanted him in high school when his good looks and swagger had intimidated her so much she hadn't been able to talk to him. And she wanted him now when he was sitting next to her looking so complicated, so human, so…

Lane.

She opened her door and stepped carefully out of the cab. Her boots found purchase as she walked to the door and unlocked it. Since her loft was over Sweet Pea Flowers, she had to unlock a door to a stairway that was next to their entrance. She unlocked the door and glanced over her shoulder at Lane.

He had his head tipped back and his mouth open, letting the snowflakes fall into it. She smiled as she stood there and watched him. He suddenly realized she was watching and her smile deepened as she noticed the flush of color on his face.

"You weren't supposed to see that," he said.

"Why not?" she asked. "I like seeing the real you. Not the one you are always so careful to show the world."

"The real me isn't all about snowflakes," he said carefully.

"I know that. But it's part of you," she said.

She opened the door and climbed up the stairs, very aware of Lane's heavy footfalls behind her. She took her time, unsure if she should have let him go first or if he might need her help. There was a small landing at the top of the stairs. She turned to see Lane had the shoulder strap for the duffel bag slung across his body, and he was using his arms to lever himself up the stairs.

His muscles bulged as he moved. He moved in a rhythm, swinging the lower half of his body as he let go of the railing and sort of jumped his way up the stairs. She could watch him all day. Biceps flexing, his face a study in concentration…he made her breath catch in her throat as she watched him move. As soon as he saw her watching him, he put his legs back on the stairs and walked up them just like she had.

"Why did you stop?" she asked.

He shrugged and winked at her.

Her heart jumped and her pulse raced faster. And she had that out-of control feeling that she got before she did something…dangerous. Dangerous? This was Lane Scott. American hero, hometown cowboy, and the only man she'd ever regretted walking away from.

"Just didn't want to show off in front of you," he said.

"I'm always impressed by you," she admitted and then felt silly for admitting it. But it was the truth. For as long as she could remember she'd been impressed with Lane Scott, and nothing she'd come to know of him in the last few days had changed that.

✯

FELICITY'S APARTMENT SMELLED like home. The couches were large and overstuffed. The exposed beams on the ceilings had been draped with lights and there was a thick carpet runner that padded each of his steps. The scent of the dinner that she'd put in the crockpot filled the entire loft space.

As he stepped over the threshold he stopped to look around. Monty's wife Risa had originally purchased the flower shop and loft apartment when she'd come to Marietta, and she rented it out now. But the place didn't seem to belong to anyone other than Felicity.

There was a medium-size Christmas tree—the one she'd purchased at the tree farm—in one corner. As she moved into the room, she stopped to flick on the tree lights. It was brightly colored. As he moved closer he realized it was decorated with handmade ornaments that if he had to guess he'd say her students had made.

She went to the large stone fireplace and set a match to the fire that had already been laid. He noticed that the mantel above the fireplace was decorated with garland. There were pictures of her parents on one end and of Copper Mountain on the other.

She hit another button and music filled the room. The sounds of Alan Jackson—one of Lane's own favorite country crooners—singing holiday favorites. She paused, looking as she so often did around him: just the tiniest bit uncomfortable.

"The bath is through there," she said, pointing to a section of the loft that was concealed by a large folding screen. The screen was painted with large hibiscus blooms in various shades of pink, orange, and yellow. A bright pop of color in the large space. The frame was draped in Christmas lights and garland.

He walked toward the screen, but stopped to look back at her. She looked nervous. Hell, he was. He liked her, wanted everything to be perfect. Wished for a second he was old Lane with two solid legs beneath him so he could pick her up and toss her over his shoulder and carry her to the fireplace to make love.

He could still pick her up but it would be dicey. She was watching him. Dammit.

"I thought you weren't keen on holiday decorating," he said. "Wasn't that why you were avoiding your mom?"

"I'm not a big fan of the way Mom does it. Everything always has to be perfect and match her motif for the year. But I do like the Christmas season—just on my own terms," she said. "What about you?"

"I don't know. My brothers and father and I tried to keep our traditions alive, but really sometimes it's hard because it just underscores the fact that Mom isn't here. Having JT and Evan makes it easier. They love Christmas and each of the women my brothers have married has brought more to our family. I think…family is what makes the holiday special for me."

She nodded. "You're so lucky, Lane."

He'd heard those words more times than most people had. Only fair when it came down to the facts of his life. He was lucky. There were many times when he truly didn't feel it. But today wasn't one of them.

Felicity had toed off her Ugg-style boots and he noticed she had reindeer socks on her feet. She'd told him that first day when she'd run into him that she didn't have the holiday spirit, but it was clear she was trying.

He was a little humbled by her attitude because today, well, today he'd been feeling sorry for himself. He'd woken in that mood and it had crept in from time to time throughout the day. Nothing wrong with that feeling. His therapists and his friends were always quick to reassure him that if they were in his prosthetic shoes they'd be the same way.

But he knew he was lucky and blessed to have the life he did. Sometimes he forgot.

"Thank you."

"You're welcome," she said. "The tub is an old-fashioned claw-foot one and it's huge so you should have plenty of room. There are bath salts and a couple of different scented bath bombs in the jars on the vanity. Do you need my help with anything?"

He dropped the duffel bag he'd borrowed from Alec on the floor and walked over to her. She stood there in her stockinged feet, shorter than he was…well not really but shorter than him at present. She tipped her head back as he stopped, leaving only a scant few inches between them. As he looked down into her eyes he felt it.

Lucky.

He leaned down and brushed his lips over hers. She sighed and tipped her head to the side, her mouth opening and her hands coming around his waist. She didn't tug him toward her; instead she took a tiny step forward until their bodies were pressed together.

He deepened the kiss and tried to shut off his mind, but

he couldn't. He wanted her. He'd had sex a few times since he'd recovered but it had been just sex. This felt different.

He liked Felicity. The way she felt in his arms made him feel…well, whole. Like the scarred parts of himself weren't there anymore. Or maybe just that they didn't matter.

He sucked her tongue deeper into his mouth as she made a soft moaning sound; she broke the kiss and licked her lips as she watched him carefully.

"I need you," he said. His voice sounded raw in the open space of her loft. The soft crooning of Alan Jackson couldn't mask the ache in his voice.

She went up on tiptoe and kissed him again. "I think I need you too."

She took his hand in hers and led him back across the loft toward the panel hiding the bathroom. He followed her, not sure what to expect but knowing he wouldn't be disappointed. Felicity was turning into his Christmas angel.

★

FELICITY HAD SCREWED up in the past by going too fast with men. Probably because she'd been so shy in high school, when she'd decided to stay in Montana and go to the university in Bozeman and live at home, she'd realized that her options were limited. She'd fallen for the first guy to pay attention to her and that had been a mistake.

She'd been trying hard to make better choices when it came to men, but she knew that there was nothing rational about her and Lane. He'd always been that cute, cocky boy who she'd regretted not kissing. Regretted not going after.

And now he was here in her home, kissing her...needing her and she didn't want to be "smart". For the first time in a good long while she wanted to just be Felicity. Follow her gut.

And that was what she was going to do.

"Sit down there," she said, nudging him toward the padded vanity bench that she kept in the corner of the bathroom. Since her apartment was a loft there was very little built-in storage space and she used the padded bench to store extra towels.

He sat down and she turned her back on him, moving to the tub and the taps. She turned on the handle of the hot water and let it run. She'd realized that the sides of the tub might be too high for Lane to get into on his own. She'd thought of that as he'd been standing in her living room. Well, she'd thought of it only when she'd started picturing him getting naked to get into the bath.

"So...we have two options," she said as she finished adjusting the temperature of the bath.

"And they are?"

"I can go and get a stool from the other room and leave you to it. Or..." She trailed off as she walked back over to him.

He had undone his belt but otherwise was still dressed as he'd been in the other room.

"Or?"

"We do this together. I help you into the tub and we share the bath," she said.

"You'd have to lift me," he said.

"I think I can do it," she returned. They were close now, her face only inches from his. She was fascinated by the different flecks of color in his eyes. And the angles of his face, that sharp blade of his nose, the fullness of his lips.

"Okay. Let's try it. But we have a third option," he said.

"What is that?"

"We bathe together and I get myself into the tub," he said.

She flushed. "Can you? I didn't mean anything by suggesting I'd help you."

He touched her face, ran his fingers along the side of her jaw down to her neck. "Yes I can. It's not very elegant but I can do it."

"I'm sorry if I offended you."

"Honey, you couldn't offend me if you tried," he said. "Every time you make a suggestion like that I feel the caring behind it. It means a lot to me that you care."

She nodded. "I do care, Lane. I don't know if it's just because it's Christmas and you seem like a nice safe spot in the storm that my mom has created or if it's regret from not pursuing things with you years ago, but I don't want to let a second chance slip by."

"Me either. I can't let this opportunity pass."

He kissed her again then. His mouth moving with assurance, kissing her deeply and strongly, and making her feel that maybe he felt the same. That maybe Lane understood where she was coming from because he was in the same position she was.

She lifted her head. And stood up. Ready for whatever might come. But she was still her same awkward self. "Do you want bath salts or the bath bomb?"

He laughed but not in an unkind way. "What scent is the bomb?"

"Home for the holidays or French lavender," she said.

"Holidays," he said.

She dropped it into the bath and then as the water edged toward the fill line, she turned off the taps. She turned to see that Lane had started disrobing and realized she was going to need to get naked too.

She pulled her sweater over her head and then pushed her jeans down her legs. She turned back to him, wearing only her matching holiday plaid underwear and bra and a pair of knee-high reindeer socks one of her students had given her last Christmas.

Lane was all the way down to his boxers and for the first time she saw him naked. His chest and arms were hugely muscled. He had a large tattoo that covered the left side of his body from his shoulder all the way down to his waist. It was…well Marietta, she thought. The large mountain range in the distance and the small cabin nestled at the foot of the mountain. There were tall pine trees and a river running through it. His body was a living canvas for their hometown.

"Is this cabin on the Scott ranch?" she asked.

She came closer to see it more clearly. She traced her fingers over the ink, following it around his body, and she noticed that his breath came in sharply as she got closer to his waist, saw his erection against the front of his underwear. She looked up at him again. Their eyes met as she stood up and took a step back.

"Yes, it is," he said, his voice husky and deep, brushing over her senses like a living thing.

"You're beautiful, Lane," she said.

Chapter Six

"You're the beautiful one," he said. Once she had adjusted the water level and taken off her clothes he caught his breath. Her back was long and smooth, curving gently into rounded hips. She glanced back over her shoulder at him and a jolt went through his body, making him tingle with need.

"Is the water level too high for you?" she asked. Her voice was softer, huskier than he'd ever heard it, brushing over his aroused senses like a live wire.

Her bangs fell forward over her face for a moment, obscuring her face from his view, and he let his gaze move over her body. From this angle he could only see the curve of her breast and the hint of a soft pink nipple. Her waist was nipped in, and there was a slight curve to her belly.

"The water is fine," he said. His own voice was loud, jarring in the silence that had built between them. He felt big, and rough, like the rancher he'd been raised to be and the solider he'd become. Felicity was everything that was soft and gentle. He wasn't.

He couldn't be.

It wasn't part of who he was. And since this was Felicity and not a woman he'd met while he was on the road, he wanted to be better than he was. He knew that he didn't want this to be for only one night and yet he'd become a one-night man.

"Lane?"

He glanced up to see her awkwardly standing there. Her legs sort of crossed to protect her feminine bits and her arms draped over her breasts. It was the most endearing thing he'd ever seen. And the concerns he had been letting build in his mind drifted away.

This was Felicity. And there wasn't another person he'd rather be with than her.

He levered himself to his stumps and then walked over toward her.

"I didn't realize you could walk without the prosthetics," she said.

"Yeah. Is it weird?" he asked. Some women he'd been with since his injury only wanted to sleep with him for the novelty of it.

But those women weren't Felicity and he was hoping that she saw him as Lane and not as a wounded vet.

"Not at all. I'm taller than you now," she said, with a grin.

"You are, but I'm still stronger and more agile," he replied.

"More agile?"

Everything about her turned him on and he knew there was no way she could miss his raging hard-on, but he also could see that she was feeling a bit shy. Teasing and joking with him to make things more…well he had no idea more what, but somehow more relaxed.

"Yeah, stand back; I might splash a little as I get into the tub," he said.

She stepped aside, forgetting her nudity and letting her arms drop to her sides as she watched him.

He put his hands on the side of the tub and lifted his entire body up off the ground. Carefully, he levered himself up over the side of the tub and into the water with a splash. He looked over at her and saw something in her eyes he was afraid to assign too much meaning to. But it looked like…well affection mixed with lust.

"Wow. That is impressive. I struggle to lift myself up on the monkey bars when the kids want me to play with them at recess."

"Well, I have always had a lot of upper body strength and I work out at the gym with Monty and Hud. Hud was afraid to really take me on at first but now he's stopped pulling his punches."

Lane was aware that he was rambling a little bit but he was nervous. She looked so good standing next to the tub and he wanted this moment to last forever. He never wanted to forget the way she looked or the scent of the bath salts or the way that she stood there hesitantly…

"I didn't really think this through. Do you want me to leave you alone?" she asked.

"No. I want you in this tub with me. Don't start being all tentative now, honey. That's not the woman you really are."

She shook her head as she walked closer to the tub and then delicately stepped into it and stood there above him. His eyes immediately went to the dark brown hair that covered her secrets and then slowly moved upward. She was perfectly formed.

Damn him.

She was gorgeous. All that he'd observed earlier seemed to be almost wrong. How could have missed how smooth her skin was or that her nipples weren't soft pink but an almost deep rose color? Her breasts were fuller than he'd thought they were. A pinkish blush started on her chest and he looked at her.

"Like what you see?" she asked.

"Very much."

She sat down between his spread legs but with her back at the end where the taps were. She pulled her knees up to her chest, careful not to touch him.

"You can't hurt me," he said. "Don't worry about touching me."

She bit her lower lip and then slowly stretched her feet toward the junction of his thighs. He took one of her feet in his hand and then the other and draped them over the tops of his thighs.

She wriggled her toes as he did so. He caressed her legs, starting at her ankles and working his way up. She didn't just sit and watch him; instead she reached for his thigh, her fingers light and a little bit cold as she touched him just under the water. She drew her hands down toward the bottom of his leg where the stump was and stopped.

"Do you feel this?"

He nodded. "On my thighs I do. But as you go lower the nerves are damaged and I don't feel as much."

She lifted her hand from him and pulled her left leg off of him, tucking it under her body as she leaned forward and lifted his leg out of the water. She studied the scarred part of his leg and then touched him gently, tracing over the skin that had healed, and then he sucked in his breath as she brushed a soft kiss against the biggest scar on his leg. She set his leg down and then shifted around to lift the other leg, which was technically an inch shorter now.

"You had more damage over here," she said.

"It was the side that took the brunt of the explosion," he said.

She kissed his leg and then shifted so she could move up his body. The tattoo that covered his left side had been done by an artist who specialized in tattoos on damaged skin. Felicity had turned him on earlier when she'd examined it and her touch had the same pronounced effect on him this time. He'd had skin grafts but the explosion had left its mark all over his body.

She touched the tattoo, her fingers moving slowly over him. She traced each of the designs until she'd examined his entire front. She drifted over him and straddled his lap again. He liked it when she sat on him that way. He wanted her. Her breasts bounced as she tried to get settled and she put her hands on his shoulders.

"I'm sorry you were hurt, Lane. I can't imagine—"

"I'm not," he interrupted her. "It was my job. It's in the past."

She chewed her lower lip and then nodded. "Did I offend you?"

He shook his head. Everyone who realized how badly injured he was felt some sort of guilt and gratitude. But the truth was he hadn't done anything special. He had been doing his job and there wasn't anything anyone could say that would convince him differently.

"I don't want you to focus on that," he said at last. "I want to be just a guy with his girl. Enjoying being young and alive."

"Me too," she said.

She leaned down, resting her forehead on his and for a long moment she stared into his eyes. Hers were so big and brown and up close he could see that there were tiny flecks of gold in her irises.

Then she squeezed his shoulders and rocked back on her heels. "Would you rather I concentrate on this?"

She scraped her fingernails down the front of his chest, lightly abrading his muscles; she ran the tips of her nails around each of his nipples, which felt weird. He hunched his shoulders and then reached up and cupped her breasts.

"I'd rather concentrate on you," he said. She fascinated him. It had been a long time since he'd slept with a woman and it was about more than need. This was desire for Felicity, not his body needing a release.

She continued caressing his body, moving her hand down his chest, teasingly following the line of hair that narrowed as it covered his abdomen and led to his groin. She ran her fingertip around his belly button and his erection jumped, brushing against her center. She rocked her hips against him and he groaned.

"Like that?" she asked with such devilish intent that he hardened even more against her.

"I do," he said. But he didn't want this to be just about what he liked. He needed to learn what she enjoyed as well.

He cupped her breasts in his hands, lifting them up as he leaned forward and took one of her nipples into his mouth. He lightly pinched the other one with his free hand. She rocked against him again. As he continued to suckle her hand drifted lower, taking him in her hand and stroking him up and down.

"I don't want to be awkward but I'm on the pill," she said.

"Good. I'm glad," he said.

She shifted on him, moving until he was poised at the entrance of her body and he lifted his head as she straddled him again. She took one of his hands in hers and knitted their fingers together before slowly lowering herself until he was fully seated inside of her.

She felt so damned good that he had clench his teeth and close his eyes to keep from grabbing her hips and just thrusting into her until he came. But he wanted this to last…at least a few more seconds.

He felt the brush of her breath over his lips and then her mouth was on his, her tongue thrusting deep into his mouth as she started to ride him. Her breasts bounced with each movement of her hips, brushing over his chest, and he brought his hands up to cup them. Rubbed his fingers over her nipples as she continued to move over him.

The water splashed and tension built inside of him. He tore his mouth from hers and took her nipple into his mouth, suckling hard as he put his hands on her hips and took control of her motions, held her hips in his hands as he started thrusting up into her.

He was so close but he wanted her with him so he slowed down, opened his eyes to look up at her. Her eyes were closed, her head back. There was a slight pink flush to her skin. Her nipples were hard and her mouth was open.

She was so gorgeous and hot and he felt his orgasm rush through him. He caressed her back and drew her down toward him, taking her mouth with his as he reached between their bodies and found her center. He flicked his finger over her pleasure spot until he felt her tightening around him.

He thrust harder and harder into her until he was empty. She rode him until his last thrust and then fell forward, collapsing against him and resting her head on his shoulder.

The water slowly stopped lapping around them and he kept her firmly anchored to him with one arm around her waist and the other around her shoulder. He didn't want to let her go.

And that made him realize he had to. Always in life the things he clung the tightest to were the ones that never failed to slip out of his grasp.

★

FELICITY HAD NEVER…WELL, never made love in a bathtub before. In fact, her ex Johnny used to like to make love with the lights off because he said her legs were too long. She didn't think that Lane had noticed. He'd made her forget about all that stuff.

There was something about Lane that just made it easy to be herself. She wasn't sure if she trusted it. Her true self had always been just a little bit left of center.

"That was…incredible," she said at last. In her mind she was still trying to process it. Her skin was still tingling, her lips felt swollen from his kisses, and as she felt him pressed against her all she could think was that she wanted him again.

"For me too," Lane said. He caught a strand of her hair and wrapped it around his finger, making it curl.

She felt a little bit awkward now that they were just lying together in the tub. She'd never bathed with anyone before and she wasn't sure what to do next. Was there some kind of protocol? Did he need to do something for his legs?

But Lane simply turned her in his arms.

"Want me to wash your hair?" he asked. His hands were on her shoulders and she was nestled between his legs. She felt his chest pressed against her back.

"I'd like that," she said.

They changed the water in the tub and then he washed her hair. His hands on her head, massaging it, felt incredible. When he was done washing her hair, they switched places and she washed his. They talked about normal things and she felt something deep inside of her shift and then settle.

Some of the doubts that she'd had about herself drifted away like the water down the drain.

When it was time to get out of the tub she wasn't sure what to do.

"So…not to be weird, but is there anything special I have to help you do to get out of the bath?" she asked.

He shook his head. "I'm good to do it. Might be easier if you were already out of the tub so that I don't have to worry about hitting you when I lift myself out."

"I know I said it before," she said as she climbed out of

the tub and reached for her towel. "But I'm really impressed with your strength."

"Why thank you, ma'am. I practice a lot and do some serious upper body training so that if my legs give out I'm still able to take care of myself."

He levered himself up and out of the tub and shifted to stand on his... "What do you call your legs?"

"Legs," he said.

"Duh. I meant the part where your prosthetics attach," she said. "Or is it just legs?"

"I call them stumps as do most. The part where my leg joins the prosthetic is called a socket on the device," he said.

He only reached the middle of her chest without his prosthetics on but he moved like he always did. He had the clothes he'd brought with him from Alec's and she left him to go to her closet and get dressed. She put on a large Christmas nightshirt and a pair of thigh-high knitted socks.

"Give me your clothes from today and I'll wash them so they'll be clean for you when you leave," she said. "I'll get dinner too."

"You don't have to wait on me," he said. "Does it bother you that I'm not wearing the prosthetics?"

"No. Nothing about you does," she said. "I like seeing you like this. I feel special—like I'm the only one who gets to see this side of you."

Then she felt silly for having said that.

"You are special, honey. Point me to the washer and I'll

toss my clothes in while you dish up supper. It smells good and I'm hungry," he said.

"I hope you like it. It's crockpot hunter's chicken. I got the recipe off Pinterest. Do guys know what that is?" she asked. "All the people I know who use it are women."

Lane laughed and the sound was deep and made her stop and smile. It was nice having him in her apartment, she thought. He came back into the main living area.

"I know what it is, but only because of hearing my sisters-in-law discuss their boards. Emma's been pinning stuff for the nursery."

"I bet she is excited," Felicity said.

"She is," Lane said. "Do you want kids?"

She looked over at him. It was something she'd thought about a lot lately. "Some day. I think I need to figure out myself before I bring a kid into the world."

Lane nodded. "I have had that thought a time or two, but then I remember Carson and how messed up he was after Raine died and he did a great job with Evan."

"Evan is awesome," Felicity said. "You're lucky to have your brothers. When it's time for you to start a family they will be a good help."

"I am blessed in my family," Lane confirmed.

"Do you want to eat at the table or sit in front of the television and watch a holiday special?"

"TV," he said. "How do you feel about a picnic in front of the fireplace?"

"Sounds perfect," she said.

Sometimes it scared her a little how in synch she and Lane seemed to be. There were times when he just got exactly what she was thinking and what she wanted. It worried her because she knew that perfect was an illusion and one that would be very hard to maintain.

But for tonight she was happy to just sit in front of the fireplace with her cowboy.

Chapter Seven

THE FIRE CRACKLED as he set his bowl aside. She wore a pair of thigh-high knitted socks and her Christmas nightshirt. Her hair was curlier than normal after their bath. Framing her heart-shaped face. She stared into the flames and he wondered what she was thinking but didn't ask.

He didn't want anything to ruin this moment for him. Even reality. The truth was he was falling for Felicity. He wasn't sure how it had started but it was there in the pit of his stomach—and like a tiny ember in his heart. Every time he looked at her, he felt that quiver of excitement all through his body. She made him…she made him forget the things that normally dominated his thoughts.

He felt complete with her. Not because of her, but because of the man he was with her. Unlike many others she seemed okay with the fact that normal wasn't really anything that anyone could achieve and it was exactly what he needed.

"You're staring at me," she said, in a soft singsong voice.

"That's because you are so pretty," he said.

She flushed. "Oh, my goodness. I can't believe you remember that," she said.

He laughed. How could he have forgotten the cute, shy girl she'd been in high school? Even then she'd had that quirk of blurting out the truth without really thinking of the consequences.

"How could I forget it? You were the first person…actually maybe the last to call me pretty," he said, stretching his arm against the back of the couch and drawing her into the curve of his body.

She lightly punched him on the chest before settling down next to him. "Was there ever a time when I wasn't a big goober?"

"I hardly think of you that way."

"You don't?"

"No, it's very refreshing to be with someone who speaks their mind the way you do," he said. He hadn't realized how refreshing until he'd come back home and found his friends trying to pretend that he was okay while ignoring his injury. And he understood where they were coming from. How difficult it was to actually talk about it. Hell, most of the time he wanted to ignore the loss of the bottom half of his legs and pretend it hadn't happened, but he couldn't.

"Well it has led to some awkward moments in my life," she said. "I bet you've never been in a situation like that."

"I've had awkward things happen," he said.

"Because of something you said?"

"Yeah. Once or twice."

She put her head on his shoulder and rolled her head to

the side to make eye contact with him. "Once or twice…that must be nice."

He laughed as he thought she might want him to. "So…what is going on with you and Christmas?"

"Nothing, why do you ask?"

"You were running from your mom and said you didn't feel the holiday spirit, but this place paints a different picture. Seems like something is bothering you."

She tucked a strand of hair behind her ear, sat up, and scotched away from him, turning to face him. She crossed her legs and put her hands on her knees as she leaned forward. "Are we doing this?"

"Doing what?"

"Sharing secrets? Because if we leave things as they are, we can be friends and holiday lovers, but if we start talking about the important things then this will change," she said. "I'm not saying I object, but I just want to make sure I'm on the same page with you."

Had she not been with another guy? He tried to figure out what she was asking but in the end had to just take her at her words. "Yes, we're doing this. But why don't we start with something easier? Thanks to living in Marietta we both know things about each other's families but we don't really know each other."

"So true. What do you want to know?" she asked.

"Christmas: fifty questions," he suggested.

"Tonight? That's a lot of information," she said.

"Not tonight. Over the entire holiday season, any time we are together we can ask a few questions. I want this to last," he said.

"Me too," she agreed.

Then she pursed her lips. "What's your favorite Christmas cookie?"

"That's a tough one to start with," he said. "Snickerdoodles are pretty good and I can't resist a frosted cut-out cookie…but my favorite are peppermint pinwheels."

"Why?" she asked. "Is it because of the taste of the cookie or something else?"

He leaned back against the couch again and realized that even simple questions could be revealing. "Part of it is the taste—I do love peppermint—but Mom used to make cookies with each of us boys on our own. It was a little one-on-one time with her. And those were the ones we always made. She'd let me add the food coloring to half the dough and the essence of mint. We used to grow it in her garden, so in the late summer we'd pick a bunch and she and I would grind it up to make a paste and get the oil to use for our Christmas cookies."

He hadn't thought of that in years. He did know that when he'd been lying in the hospital in Germany, waiting for transport back to the US, one of the nurses had brought in a few sprigs of peppermint and left them on his nightstand.

He'd learned later that it had been because of a few words from his brother Trey. For Lane it had felt like his mom had been close and the philosophical part of him wanted to believe it was partly due to the fact that he'd needed her for the journey back to the land of the living.

Felicity crawled over to him and wrapped her arms around him, straddling his lap. "That is the sweetest story. I love it."

He wrapped his arms around her and held her close to his chest.

☆

FELICITY ENJOYED THE evening with Lane a lot. She told him her favorite cookie—chocolate chip—learned that he knew the words to every verse of "Joy to the World" and thought that mulled wine was the worst-tasting drink he'd ever had.

She told him about getting mixed up when she was little and thinking that the "I Saw Mommy Kissing Santa Claus" was truly about Mommy having an affair with the big guy. And that she didn't like eggnog.

As the embers in the fire began to die down, she started feeling awkward again and really was trying to keep her mouth closed. But she was tired. Lane hadn't put his prosthetics back on after their bath and lovemaking, so they were both just cuddled on the sheepskin rug that she'd ordered online from IKEA when she'd first moved into the apartment. She had a plaid blanket that she always put out a Christmas that they'd draped over their laps.

"Want some hot chocolate?"

"Depends on what kind it is," he said.

She wasn't very sophisticated when it came to her hot chocolate at home. "Swiss Miss."

He nodded. She got up and went to the kitchen and heard Lane moving around behind her. He wore a pair of sweat pants with the bottoms cut off so they rested on his legs just before where his knee would have been. His flannel button-up shirt was a blue plaid color that made his eyes seem even brighter than normal.

"Quick fire round," she called from the kitchen to distract herself as she boiled water for their hot chocolate. "I can't believe you love Swiss Miss too."

Lane was walking around her living room on his "stumps". It was interesting to see him relaxed and being himself. She noticed that he'd stopped in front of her Christmas tree and seemed to be reading all of the ornaments. Her students often wrote her messages on them.

"Sage's is the best for hot chocolate but really nothing beats the little pack with those ridiculously tiny marshmallows."

"Agreed. So are you ready?" she asked, pouring the hot water into one of the matching mugs painted in red and green stripes. She left an inch on the top of the mug, stirred the powder until it dissolved, and then added milk before taking a can of Reddi-wip from the fridge and squirting it on top of the chocolate. She gave each mug a sprinkle of

Christmas-colored sugar and then turned to find Lane watching her.

"Well that is some fancy Swiss Miss."

She flushed a bit. "Too much?"

"Nah, it's perfect." He walked over to her and it was odd at first for him to be only chest high. His features were relaxed; in his blue eyes she thought she saw a hint of happiness. She handed him his mug and he took it from her, walking back over to the blanket in front of the fireplace where they'd been sitting.

"Quick fire," he said. "We each fire off three questions in turn. Sound good?"

She carefully sat down and then took a sip of her hot chocolate. Her favorite part of drinking it this way was when the whipped cream melted in her mouth as the hot liquid hit it. She opened her eyes to find Lane sitting next to her, watching her.

She licked her lips.

His eyes tracked the movement.

She set her cup down as a slow heat began to build inside of her. She was trying to play it cool but there was no way to do that around Lane. He was seriously built and just everything about him made her think of being back in his muscly arms. Feeling the warmth of his naked body against hers as he moved over her.

"Favorite Christmas TV show?" she blurted out.

He gave her a knowing grin and took his time settling

back on the blankets. He moved with surety and confidence, which she had come to expect.

"*Santa Claus is Comin' to Town*," he said. "Yours?"

"*Grinch*—the animated one not the Jim Carrey one."

He arched one eyebrow at her. "Midnight mass or the kids' evening mass with the nativity?"

"Nativity—and not just because my students are usually in it. I like celebrating the holiday with kids."

"Same," he said.

His eyes were intense as he watched her and she was on the cusp of asking him to spend the night. Which she thought might be too soon considering they'd only had one date. "Snowy kisses or mistletoe ones?"

"If I'm kissing you: both," he said. "But otherwise snowy because I'm kissing someone I want to and not because of tradition."

"So…" she said. She wanted to know if he was going to spend the night. She wasn't sure if he even had a job…that wasn't true, she knew he traveled around and participated in sporting events for wounded vets. She'd heard that he gave talks at schools and she knew he spent a lot of time at Ka-Pow, which he co-owned with Hudson and Monty Davison. But did he have someplace to be on Monday morning?

"So?"

"Ugh, you're going to make me be awkward again, aren't you?" She took her empty cocoa mug and placed it on the end table. "Are you spending the night?"

He choked a little on his sip. "Do you want me to?"

She didn't know. The last man to spend the night had been Johnny and that hadn't ended so well for either one of them. It wasn't that she was bad at relationships—really, she didn't think anyone was good at them—it was more that she was all or nothing. She could keep it fun and light if he left; but if he spent the night and began to do it on a daily basis, she'd start to get really attached.

And she didn't know about other women but she seemed unable to stop herself from building those hearth and home fantasies around a guy when they were serious.

"I guess that's not a yes."

She chewed her lower lip. "It's not a no. I just have school in the morning and I'm not sure what your routine is. I don't want to make things weird."

He rolled his shoulders, stretching the flannel shirt he wore over his chest, and she sighed. He was seriously built and the last thing she wanted to do was to crawl into her bed alone. But she also didn't want to ruin this. The fun of this thing that she'd started with Lane.

She could sort of be herself with him and he didn't seem to mind. He was funny and sexy but there was more going on under the surface than he let on. And she wanted to be the one who was there for him.

She groaned.

"What?"

"Nothing."

No way was she going to admit that she was already bonding with him. Thinking of ways to blend their lives together... They'd had one date and slept together. That was it. Any other woman would...but she wasn't any other woman and she could only be herself. More's the pity.

"I do want you to stay," she admitted. "But only if you want to."

☆

LANE WOKE TO the smell of coffee and the sound of the shower. He rolled over and stared bleary-eyed at the clock. It was six a.m. He knew where he was. He hadn't slept well—afraid that if he allowed himself to sleep he might dream, and his dreams weren't always pleasant. So instead he'd been tossing and turning all night. When he'd finally drifted off...she'd gotten out of bed to start her day.

Did he need more proof that he wasn't ready for this? That normal was still a damned long way off?

He could have done without it.

He noticed she'd put his prosthetics near the chair in the corner of her bedroom and draped his cleaned clothes—she'd insisted on washing and drying them last night—next to the chair. He got out of bed and walked over to the chair, carrying his coffee with him.

Monday.

There had a been a time when he'd first woken up in DC that he'd had to remind himself each morning what day it was. Everything in his life had blurred together until he no longer felt like he was living, but that had passed.

He was closer and closer every day to being…just like everyone else.

Or so he'd thought until last night.

Not the lovemaking or fire-watching part. The sleeping part.

How was he going to convince anyone he was normal—hell, himself? He was the only person he was interested in convincing and he was his harshest critic. He always had been. He set his coffee on the floor next to the chair and levered himself up onto the chair. He pulled his prosthetics toward him and put them on. He was standing fastening his jeans when Felicity walked back into the room.

"Morning," she said. Her hair was wet and curled around her face but she was dressed and had applied her makeup. She gave him a smile but he could tell she hadn't gotten much more rest than he had the night before.

He wanted to say something. Anything to explain what he'd been going through, but talking about it would just make it worse. He didn't know if he was ever going to relax enough to sleep through the night with her.

"Morning," he said, "Thanks for the coffee."

She nodded and went across the room, stopping at a large wicker basket to drop off her dirty clothes. "I need to blow-dry my hair and then I'll be ready to go."

Both of them ignoring the very large problem. How

could he feel comfortable enough to have sex with her but not relax enough to actually sleep?

The answer came to him in a rush. He'd had sex with other women. He knew his limitations and his expectations with this new body. But sleeping…he hadn't slept with anyone since his injury.

He walked into the kitchen and poured out his coffee. He hadn't thought about this being a first until this very moment. And while he felt a bit better knowing that things could only improve, he wasn't sure if Felicity would want to be along for the journey with him.

He'd recovered physically from the injuries he'd sustained. He'd covered his scars in tattoos and learned to walk in these new limbs, but it was sobering to realize that he was still mentally recovering. He thought he was long past it and he was a little bit pissed to realize he wasn't.

He kept thinking normal was just around the corner but this morning was showing him that normal might be a long way off. And was it fair to start something with Felicity when he wasn't sure?

Hell, could he walk away?

"Lane?"

He looked up at her when she called his name. She was staring at him and chewing her lip. She looked nervous.

"Yes?"

"Sorry if I kept you up last night," she said at last. "I was so afraid of jarring you or hurting you; I tried to lie still."

He shook his head and walked over to her, took her in his arms and hugged her tight. It was a first for both of them. That was why it hadn't been better for both of them.

"I was nervous too. I haven't slept with anyone since I got back to the US," he said.

She tipped her head back and gave him a shy smile. "I'm glad I was the first. We'll do better next time…right?"

Next time. Well she was willing to try again. He knew he needed to be too. He liked her. It wasn't just sex. Or the fact that it was Christmas and he was alone. It was Felicity and he wanted this to last.

"Right," he said. "Now let's get you to school."

Chapter Eight

FELICITY NORMALLY WALKED to school quickly. It was cold and at times she hated the snow, but it wasn't that far from her apartment on Main Street to the elementary school. It took more time and effort to warm the car up—and sometimes shovel the alleyway—than to just walk. But as they got downstairs, she wondered if Lane would rather drive. Or if he'd say good-bye here. He could do that.

She felt awkward and realized he probably did too. She was ready for some time away to put it all into perspective. She'd spent the entire night lying next to him, wanting to ask him questions but staying silent in case he was finally sleeping.

"Do you want me to scrape the ice from your car?" he asked.

"No. I'm going to walk to school." Her school bag was heavy, loaded down with some cookies she'd baked on Saturday for her students, as well as some Christmas decorations that she had for the kids to color during their downtimes during the school day.

She'd never really thought about what she wanted to be

when she grew up, but she had to admit being a teacher suited her. She loved it.

She was trying to distract herself from Lane and doing an okay job of it. From the corner of her eye she watched him. Every time she looked at him she was reminded of the fact that he hadn't kissed her since last night. She remembered the feel of his body against hers and her lips started tingling. She wanted to kiss him again.

He settled his knitted skullcap on his head and pulled on his shearling coat. He looked at her and she caught her breath. His face was all angles and masculine beauty and she remembered how he'd looked naked in her apartment last night.

Mine.

She wanted to claim him as hers but if last night had shown her anything it was that they still had a long way to go before they were a couple. They both had things they were hiding. Both were trying to make things seem as good as they could while sweeping the dirt of real life under the carpet.

She knew better than to start anything with him while she was in this state. In the past she'd always had a boyfriend or a group of girlfriends to blunt the attentions but this year…she'd isolated herself. Drawn further and further into her shell to avoid facing the truth. She'd changed and she wasn't sure how to deal with it.

She wanted to claim Lane but she wasn't sure she had the

right to. He'd told her she was the first person he'd slept with since his injury and she knew that was significant. She wanted to be worthy of it. Not just someone who was running from loneliness and desperately clinging to this hot as sin cowboy who'd seen more pain than anyone should in one life.

He wasn't hers.

But she wanted him to be. Now she had to convince herself she deserved him.

"I usually stop at the Diner for a quick breakfast. Want to join me?"

"If I do everyone will know we're a couple," he said. "The gossips won't miss it. Are you ready for that?"

Was she? "Yes. Are you?"

"I wouldn't have spent the night with you otherwise," he said. He walked over to her and held out his hand. She joined her hand with his and they walked out of the alleyway.

It was funny because she couldn't let herself relax. If people knew they were dating then she'd have to be better than she had been until now. Not herself but the kind of woman that people would expect Lane to date.

He was a hero. A man who'd been through so much and come out on the other side even stronger than before. And Felicity knew she was weak. She was as far from perfect as one woman could get.

She slipped on a patch of ice; grabbed Lane's arm and he

held her steady. Not falling but keeping them both upright. She tipped her head back, looking into those gorgeous blue eyes of his. She saw something in his expression. Determination, of course, but something else she couldn't define.

"Sorry about that."

"Don't be. Are you okay?" he asked.

"No," she said. "I'm not sure anyone is going to think I'm special enough to be with you, Lane. You are—"

"A guy," he said. "I'm just like everyone else where it counts and maybe I'm not special enough to be your guy. But you know what, honey? I'm going to try. This might not work but it certainly isn't going to be because one of us isn't good enough."

She wanted to argue. He didn't know her or how she sometimes hid, but he had a point. It didn't matter what anyone else thought. She couldn't be the girlfriend she thought people expected him to have; she could only be herself and for Lane it seemed that was enough. So she had to let it be for now.

He led the way around the block to Main Street and she stood there looking at the early morning with the inky fingers of dawn slowly receding. The Christmas lights sparkled in the windows of all of the shops. It looked magical.

She realized that Lane stood stock-still next to her as well. He reached for her hand and held it in his gloved one.

"I missed this when I was in the Middle East. Small

towns like Marietta aren't the norm over there and I thought…well, when I signed up to join the Marines I thought that I wanted to be as far from here as a man could be, but then damn me if I didn't miss it."

She squeezed his hand in hers. "I always miss it when I go away. There's just something special about this town…maybe because it's ours."

"Ours," he repeated. "I like that."

★

The Main Street Diner was rustic and charming. Of course, she'd been coming in here since her feet would dangle as she sat in one of the booths that lined the room. Her father had always taken her and her sister, Andrea, to breakfast on Saturdays so her mom could catch up from the week and sleep in.

Flo was at the counter and waved at them as she listened to Earl talking to her about the time he'd been snowed in town for three days back in the '40s. Lane moved to one of the tables near the center of the room and held the chair out for Felicity to sit down.

She did so after setting her school bag on the floor next to the table. Lane took his seat and then they both looked at each other and smiled. They'd made the decision to do this and now she felt kind of silly for making such a big deal about it.

It wasn't as if people were going to be able to guess

they'd slept together because they were having breakfast in town.

"Aren't you going to be in trouble for eating here?" Flo asked as she came over with two ceramic coffee mugs in one hand and a pot of coffee in the other. She set them on the table and poured each of them a cup.

"Nah, Lucy doesn't mind where I eat breakfast. Besides she says her favorite breakfast is the breakfast casserole served here," Lane said.

Felicity had forgotten that Lucy DeMarco Scott owned a breakfast-only restaurant out near the highway in the newish strip mall. It was in the same area as Ka-Pow—the martial arts gym Lane, his brother Hudson, and his best friend Monty owned.

"What brings you to town so early in the morning?" Flo asked.

"Breakfast casserole," Lane said with a wink.

Felicity smiled. He was smooth, but Flo loved to gossip and she wasn't one to be easily distracted.

"I got your order, boy," Flo said. "What about you, Felicity?"

"French toast, please," Felicity said. "Thank you, Flo."

"You're welcome, hon," she said. As she walked away she looked back over her shoulder at Lane. "I saw your truck in the alley this morning."

She went behind the counter and Lane started laughing. "Didn't think about that. Does it bother you?" he asked

Felicity.

"Not at all," she said, but inside she was very aware that it had been a long time since she'd dated anyone…well six months. That wasn't long. But to her it had felt even longer because of everything that had happened with her ex. "What about you?"

"Nope. I really don't care too much what other people think. I'm not saying that was always the case, but war and my injuries put everything in perspective."

He humbled her. Her head was filled with the same self-deprecating thoughts as always but he'd faced some real scary shit in his life. Emotional baggage from her ex didn't seem to hold a candle to anything he had going on.

"I guess it would. I wonder sometimes if never leaving Marietta has made me stuck in my ways."

"In what way?"

"Just that I see things as they always are. Nothing really changes here too much and I wonder if I'm stuck too."

"Do you feel stuck?" he asked, his bright blue gaze catching hers, and she felt like he could see all the way to her soul.

She did feel stuck. Not by the place but by her own circumstances. She could only see her life the way it had always been. Lane was different though. She wanted to be better. To be the kind of woman who could match his strengths, but she was very afraid she never would be.

She shrugged instead of answering and noticed that someone had turned on the music for the restaurant. Families started coming in for a quick breakfast and Felicity was glad because she didn't want to really talk any more about herself.

"Quick fire," Lane said. "Presents on Christmas Eve or Christmas morning?"

"Morning but up early," she said.

"How early?"

"Five a.m. and Andrea and I always spend the night at our mom's so we both are there to open then," she said. "What about you?"

"Morning. But we drive out to the ranch at about ten and open them then," Lane said.

"Angel or star on top of the tree?" Felicity asked after taking a sip of her coffee.

"Star," Lane said. "My mom made the star we use now and decorated it with pictures of my brothers on the points and in the middle is a photo of my mom and dad. You?"

She loved the idea of that personalized star on the top of the tree. Nothing like that would have ever graced her mom's tree.

"An angel," Felicity said. "Mom special ordered it from Germany. It's a handblown glass one."

"I bet it's beautiful," Lane said.

"It is. But I like the sound of that star on the top of your tree. When is the picture from?"

"It's all of our high school graduation photos now. When we were growing up she used to change them out each year,"

Lane said.

She was envious, she realized. She wanted to be a part of a family like the Scotts. Flo brought their breakfast and they both ate while discussing the gingerbread competition that was held every year in town. It had been judged the night of the Stroll but all of the entries were on display in town.

Lane paid for breakfast and when they stepped outside he pulled her into his arms and kissed her.

"We survived breakfast in town," he said, taking her hand and leading her up the street toward the school.

Her lips tingled. She wanted to be cautious and not fall headlong into anything with Lane, but it was hard not too. He was doing everything right as far as she was concerned.

★

LANE ENJOYED THE walk with Felicity. For a while now he'd been thinking that there was something he had been missing to make Marietta feel like home again. He was starting to think that it might be her.

That was dangerous thinking. He knew that a woman couldn't be the answer to his problems. That the emptiness came from inside of him. Something that surgeries and state-of-the-art prosthetics couldn't fix. But this morning after breakfast at the Diner and conversation with Felicity, he almost wanted to believe it could be.

It had snowed overnight and there was some fresh powder on the playground. His prosthetics were solid and he'd had a lot of practice time to get used to keeping his balance on snow and ice. But he couldn't just walk, he had to pay attention to what he was doing. He was aware that for the rest of his life he would have to do that.

Felicity was quiet next to him. Like she had been last night, lying next to him in bed. She was a ball of contradictions and every time he thought he had her figured out, a new wrinkle popped up.

"I'm sorry I had to get you up so early," she said. "Thanks for walking me to school."

Lane was feeling...well nostalgic doing it. When he'd been in school, since they were ranch kids and not townies, his mom had driven them and he'd always sort of wanted to walk to school with his town friends.

"This is something I've always wanted to do."

She gave him a wry look. "You've got some weird things on your wish list."

He shrugged. "What's on yours?"

"I don't know," she said, but there was a quiet tone to her voice that let him know she had a few hard and fast things on her list.

"Don't get shy now, Felicity. I'm used to you blurting out things."

"Yeah, but this one is really personal and we're barely dating," she said.

"Family?"

"Yeah. Kids and marriage and that's not something that

anyone advises a woman to tell a man when they've just started sleeping together."

"Well, you can tell me. I hope…well it's probably too soon for that. But you and I have a connection, honey, and maybe I'll end up being the man you have that family with," he said.

"Maybe," she said.

In his mind's eye he could picture having a passel of kids with Felicity. They'd be hellions just like he'd been and they'd have that penchant for honesty that she did. Maybe a mix of her dark hair and his blue eyes…

She slowed as they approached the school. He turned to her and she started to speak but stopped when she spotted something over his shoulder.

"We can't talk now…I really wanted to leave early because the O'Neils are going through a divorce and Candi had to take a job in Bozeman, so she drops the boys off early. They are safe enough but it's cold and the oldest is only ten."

He wanted to know more about what she thought about the two of them, but they were at school and there were two kids huddled outside waiting.

"Is that Dev O'Neil?" Lane asked.

"Yeah. I think he was a year or two ahead of us in school," Felicity said. "He and Candi have been married since graduation but they hit a rough patch."

"I'm sorry to hear that. What are the boys' names?"

"Eddie and Carl," Felicity said.

The boys were huddled together near the entrance to the school. They had a thermos of hot chocolate they were sharing.

"Morning, boys," Felicity said as she and Lane approached.

"Morning, Miss Danvers," the elder boy said.

"Boys, this is Mr. Scott. Lane, this is Eddie and Carl."

"Hiya, boys. How's it going?" Lane asked.

"Good. I lost a tooth this weekend," Carl said, smiling to show a missing bottom tooth.

"Just in time," Felicity said. "I'll put you up front during the Christmas concert so you can be seen when we sing 'All I Want For Christmas'."

"Yay! That's what I was hoping for," Carl said. "Daddy said he lost his front tooth right before Christmas when he was my age."

"I think I remember that," Felicity said, as she unlocked the door and punched in some security codes. Lane held the door open for her and the boys to enter. The boys moved down the hall and settled on the floor outside the door of Carl's classroom.

"Do they just sit and wait?"

"Sometimes, but not this morning. I need some help, boys. Want to help me?" Felicity called to them.

"Yes, ma'am. We love to help," Eddie said.

Lane watched Felicity with the boys and realized that she was very good with them. She led the way into her classroom where she had them help her fold printed books with lyrics for Christmas carols on them.

Lane took a seat next to Carl and helped out as well. Eddie was very serious and when they'd finished folding all of the booklets, she gave the boys each a chocolate chip cookie that she'd brought with her to school in a sealed container.

He heard voices in the hallway and realized that other students and teachers were arriving. He looked over at Felicity, mouthing the word *good-bye* as he left her classroom. He was stopped by a few of the students who knew him, and his young nephews hugged him when they saw him.

"What are you doing here?" Evan asked.

"Just helping Miss Danvers with a few things this morning," Lane said.

"Is she your girlfriend, Uncle Lane?" JT asked. "You were with her at our house yesterday."

"I'm working on it," Lane said.

"Told ya," JT said to Evan. "Now you owe me a Coke."

He tousled his nephews' hair and they both ran up the hallway toward their classrooms. He watched them go, noticing that Felicity was standing in the doorway to her room. She'd heard him talking to the boys.

She gave him a smile but it seemed forced and he wondered if she was truly reluctant to be his girlfriend or if something else was going on with her.

Chapter Nine

"So…" Hudson said as Lane walked into the back office of Ka-Pow later that morning. He'd gone by his own house and changed into his workout clothes before coming to the gym he co-owned with his brother and his best friend Monty. Monty and Risa were out of town visiting Monty's dad in San Diego and wouldn't be back until next week.

"So?"

"Just wondering where you were last night," Hud said. "Don't bother saying you were at home because I went by this morning to pick you up and you weren't there."

"I wasn't going to say I was home when clearly I wasn't," Lane said.

"So…"

"I was at Felicity's." He walked past his brother who stood near the coffee station they had set up in the office. He reached around Hud to pour himself a cup of what smelled like Santa's Christmas Blend, something that Emma Jean had ordered for Hud. His brother liked cinnamon and vanilla in his coffee. Lane preferred his plain but had gotten used to drinking the blend while he was at work.

"Well, well, well," Hudson said. "That's interesting. You haven't spent the night with a gal since…well, since when?"

"None of your damn business, that's when," Lane said.

"Are you kidding? It is so my business. Since we work together you have to talk to me," Hud said as he sat down on the counter next to the coffee station and watched Lane add milk to his coffee mug.

"I think you are watching too much girly TV with your wife, Hud. We don't talk about shit like that," Lane said.

"Hell, I know. But I need to think about something other than the baby, Lane. Emma is doing well but I'm freaking out a bit. I'm not sure I'm ready to be a dad. Remember how Carson was? Remember how much Evan cried? And Lord knows Emma's probably going to be the best damned mother in the history of mothering but I'm not too sure I can hold up my end," Hudson said. He hopped off the counter and walked over to the window where he stared out at the snow-covered back parking lot.

He hadn't seen Hudson like this. Ever. Hudson was his brother with all the confidence and bravado. Lane had always thought of channeling his inner Hud when he needed to be a bad ass. But that was when he was fighting. This was babies and family. Things that typically they weren't very good at.

Except his brothers had been changing. "You're going to be great."

"How do you figure?" Hudson asked, without turning

around.

"I reckon Dad has never once worried about being a decent parent and we both know he's no great shakes at it. But you are thinking about it, already trying to be the best, and I've never known you to fail at anything," Lane said. "Not when you set your mind to it."

"Fair enough. But that doesn't stop me from feeling slightly sick when I think about a baby. I mean I didn't even hold JT or Evan when they were little. They were too tiny and I was afraid I'd break them. What am I going to do? Emma's bound to notice if I don't hold ours."

Lane looked at his brother and wondered what to say. He didn't have much experience with children other than his nephews. He took a sip of his coffee and remembered the last night with Felicity. How awkward and unbearable it had felt while he'd been going through it. "Here's what I know: nothing is easy. But you adjust to it. I bet when you left home it was scary and you might have wished you could turn around, but you didn't. You just kept moving forward and figuring it out as you went along. I think that's what it's going to be like with you and Emma and the baby."

Hud turned to face him, giving him a look that was filled with affection. "When'd you get to be so smart, Lane?"

"I think I always was. Everyone knows I got looks and brains."

Hud shook his head as he sat down at his desk and turned on his computer. "Boy, you must have gotten hit pretty hard in Afghan because it has made you think some crazy-ass shit. Everyone knows I got all that and some swagger thrown in. Just ask Emma."

Lane smiled at his brother as he moved to his own desk in the corner. "She's prejudiced, Hud. That doesn't count."

"You're wrong. I'm older, and that is the end of that. Do you want to teach the first class today or do you want me to cover it?" Hudson asked.

"Don't care," Lane answered absently as he read an email that had come in from his former CO. He had been invited to a dinner in DC at the end of the week. The get-together was to honor those who had recently recovered and the speaker they'd had lined up couldn't come.

"Damn," Lane said under his breath. He wouldn't turn it down but he had wanted to stay in Marietta and woo Felicity. But duty called and though he was a retired Marine he knew he'd never fail to answer the call when the Corps needed him.

"What?"

"I have to go to DC for a few days."

"It's no big thing. I can cover your classes," Hudson said.

"I wasn't worried about you, dumbass."

"Who were you—oh, Felicity," his brother said. "So it's serious then?"

Lane scrubbed a hand over his face. He really didn't want to have this conversation with his brother. "It could be. I'm not done sorting it out yet."

"Maybe a few days away will put it all in perspective," Hudson said. "I know when Emma went back to Nashville it changed my way of thinking."

"It didn't change it," Lane pointed out. "Just made you realize you were being a jackass."

"Well, there is that," Hudson said. "Maybe DC will do that for you."

Lane didn't think he needed a trip out of state to sharpen his thoughts where Felicity was concerned. He liked her and if last night had shown him anything, it was that he wanted to impress her. But he would miss her while he was gone. Would she miss him?

☆

ANDREA STOPPED BY the school on her way home from Bozeman. She worked in the marketing department of a sporting goods store. Her sister had always seemed…well, charmed. She made the right choices at the right time and everyone always liked her.

"Got time for a drink at the Graff before we go to Mom's for dinner?" Andrea asked as Felicity was packing up her bag at the end of the day. This time of year she was struggling to keep the kids focused on work and ensure they enjoyed the holidays. When she'd been younger Christmas had felt so magical, which was probably why she struggled so much now.

"Sure. What's up?" she asked her sister. She needed a distraction since Lane had texted her—texted, not called—to tell her he was going to be in DC for the rest of the week and that he'd be back in town next Monday.

"Nothing, just wanted to enjoy a little sister time," Andrea said. "Plus I heard a rumor that you and Mr. Lane Scott are dating. I thought surely that's not true; my sister who is only eighteen months older than I am would surely have told me something that important."

Felicity rolled her eyes. "I'm older. That means I get to decide what to tell you."

"So is it true?"

Felicity didn't know. She would have said yes on Monday but now that it was Thursday and Lane was in DC…she wasn't sure. "We haven't really talked about labels."

"Labels?" Andrea asked. "That sounds like a story and a half. What else do you need to do before we can get out of here?"

"Just lock up. I've got everything in my bag," Felicity said. "I walked over from my place."

"I figured. I'll drive us to the Graff. I'd park at Mom's but then she'd come with us for drinks and we'd have to talk about whatever holiday event she wants us to participate in this week," Andrea said. "I'm sorry I ditched you for the Stroll."

"No, you're not," Felicity said as they got into Andrea's Kia Soul and her sister drove them to the Graff.

"I'm not. It was nice to be in LA for a few days."

"I want to hear all about your trip," Felicity said, taking her clutch wallet from her bag as they left the vehicle and headed into the hotel. They headed for the bar without saying anything else and Andrea spotted a table in the back and made a beeline for it.

Felicity followed her sister. Once they were seated and had both ordered drinks—a gin and tonic for Andrea, sauvignon blanc for Felicity—Andrea propped her elbows on the table and leaned in. "Okay, spill."

"Ugh."

"Ugh? You should be all rosy and glowing and excited to talk about your new man. I know Lane is nicer than your ex."

Felicity didn't want to give Andrea the wrong impression but she also didn't want her sister to know that once again she was screwing up left and right. "He is. He's great. It's just that I'm not sure of anything."

"Like what?" Andrea asked. The waitress delivered their drinks and as soon as she was out of earshot, her sister leaned in closer. "Did you sleep with him?"

Felicity remembered that night in her bed—both of them lying so still next to each other so as not to disturb the other one. Sleeping…not really. And she remembered the tub. How perfect it had been between them. Sure she'd been afraid it would be weird because she'd do or say something to make it awkward, but it hadn't been. Because Lane was so hot and sexy. He hadn't given her a chance to feel shy at all.

"Oh my gosh. You totally did. Okay so why are you being all weird now?" Andrea said.

"I didn't say—"

"You turned like fifty shades of red. You'd only blush like that if it was a night to remember."

Felicity took a sip of her wine and then leaned back in the booth. "I don't know what is going on right now. He got called out of town on Monday. He texted me to let me know, didn't call, so I'm not sure what is going to happen when he comes back."

"He texted you?" Andrea asked.

"Yeah, that seems like he wants to put some distance between us, doesn't it?" Felicity asked.

"What did the text say?" Andrea countered. "Give me your phone."

"When did you get to be so bossy?" Felicity asked.

"Since forever. You know I'm the bossy one. Give me your phone," Andrea repeated.

Felicity handed her phone to her sister, who knew her password and keyed it in to unlock the screen. She knew Andrea's as well. They both used their dad's birthday. Not exactly the safest code but Felicity wasn't hiding anything on her phone.

Andrea scrolled through the messages, sipping her drink.

"Uh, sis, I think he texted you because he thought you'd be in class. And you responded with a thumbs up emoji…and that's it. Never texted him again."

"Well, what if he texted because he wanted to cool things down?" Felicity said. She hadn't known how to respond so she'd left it.

"I don't think that's it," Andrea said. "Want me to find out?"

"Yes, but I don't know how you'd do that," Felicity said. Andrea was pretty good friends with Lucy, Lane's sister-in-law.

"I just asked him," Andrea said.

"What?! Give me back my phone," Felicity said.

Andrea slid it back across the table and she saw the dancing dots that indicated Lane was replying to her.

> Andrea had texted to Lane: *Hey, I was in class the other day when I got this and wasn't sure if you left because you wanted to or had to.*

Andrea had asked what Felicity had been too scared to. What if he said wanted to? What then? Well, at least she'd know.

> **Lane:** *Had to. The speaker at a veterans' event canceled and I was asked to fill in. I thought you might be glad I was gone.*
>
> **Felicity:** *No. I miss you*
>
> **Lane:** *Me too. I'll be back on Monday. Want to have dinner then?*
>
> **Felicity:** *Yes. Be safe in DC. Have fun.*
>
> **Lane:** *You too.*

She put her phone on the table and looked up to find Andrea staring at her.

"Well?"

"He misses me too."

"So you are dating," Andrea said.

"We are," Felicity confirmed.

☆

BAKING COOKIES WAS one of her favorite things to do. Lane had been invited to Washington DC for some kind of award and had been gone for three days. It was silly to think how much she missed him. Three weeks ago he'd been a stranger and now he was so important that she was making peppermint pinwheels in her kitchen so that when he came home, she'd have them waiting for him.

But she did miss him. Since Andrea had texted him for her the other day, she and Lane had been doing their quick-fire Christmas questions via text. The latest one was about Christmas sweaters. Ugly or traditional? She had voted for ugly and Lane had agreed, saying a Christmas sweater wasn't worth wearing unless it had something hideously tacky crocheted on the front of it.

She shook her head. Lane was so different from the other men in her life. He was definitely a lot nicer than her ex who'd always found fault with everything she did and said. And way different than her own dad who'd been doting but never seemed to really understand who she was. Just saw her as one of his "girls".

But Lane…well, she'd been more herself with him than she had been with anyone else. Mainly because he made her feel like it was okay. And she knew she had flaws and baggage and that there were things that she would need to tell him if they continued dating, but for now she was enjoying him and the holidays.

She had The Carpenters' Christmas CD playing on her old CD player that had featured prominently in her bedroom when she'd been growing up. She glanced over at the machine, remembering when her dad had taken her to Billings to pick it out. It seemed so long ago and yet like it was yesterday when she, Andrea, and her father had made the trip.

She missed him.

Her stomach ached as she thought about the fact that it was almost ten years that he'd been gone. And though she had been avoiding her mom because she didn't want to get roped into doing one more thing during the holiday season, she suddenly really needed to talk to her. She reached for her cell phone and dialed her mom's number.

"Hiya, sweetie," her mom said as she answered the phone on the first ring.

"Hi, Mom," Felicity said. "I'm baking cookies and wondered if you wanted to come and help me."

"I'd love to. I was wrapping presents at the church, but I'm almost done. What kind of cookies are we making?"

"Well, peppermint pinwheels and I thought maybe peanut butter," Felicity said.

"Dad's favorite…who likes the peppermint ones?" her mom asked.

"Lane. He's out of town and I thought it might be nice to have them for him when he gets back," Felicity said.

"That's a great idea. I have some other goodies that you can use to make him a basket. I'll swing by the house and pick them up on my way to your place. Do you have all the ingredients?"

"I do," she said. She wasn't really sure she wanted to make a big basket for Lane, but what the heck. She missed her mom and her dad tonight. "Thank you, Mom."

"For what, honey?"

"Just coming when I called."

"I always will," she said.

"I know," Felicity replied, but sometimes she felt like she was disappointing her mom. Sometimes it seemed that Felicity was so opposite to her mother…it was hard to live up to the woman her mom was. "That's why I was thanking you."

"Are you okay?" her mom asked.

"Yeah, I was thinking about dad and just missing him and all."

"I'll be right over," her mom said, disconnecting the call.

Felicity looked around her apartment and noticed the boots she'd left lying by the door and that her school bag was flung in the middle of the floor, as were her coat and scarf.

She tidied up the house and found Lane's scarf.

She hadn't realized he'd left it behind when he'd spent the night. She lifted it up and wrapped it around her neck. It smelled of Lane's cologne and of cinnamon. She missed him.

There was a knock on the door and she took Lane's scarf off and hung it on a peg before opening the door. Her mom and sister hurried inside. Both of them bringing the cold air with them and lots of talking. Andrea hugged her and then went to the kitchen to mix up some of her "world famous" peppermint martinis.

"Sweetie, your place looks so beautiful and homey. I love the way you have decorated this year," her mom said, hugging her close.

"Really?"

"Yes, of course I do," her mom said.

"I was worried it might not be…perfect," Felicity said. Her mom always seemed to have such high standards for everything.

"Nothing's perfect. I know I get a little crazy at the holidays and it's been pointed out to me that I can be a little over the top, but never think you aren't just right the way you are. Besides we all have different things we love that make the holidays special for us," Mom said.

"Like my special martinis," Andrea called from the kitchen.

"And Dad's peanut butter cookies," Mom said.

"And family," Felicity said, realizing how blessed she was to have her mom and sister with her.

Chapter Ten

LANE WAS TIRED and his mouth hurt from smiling as he landed in Bozeman. The crew had been very gracious as they always were. He made a lot of flights in and out of Montana and the crew knew him pretty well now. It was late afternoon and he'd asked Hud to pick him up from the airport because after sitting for so long he didn't relish the thought of driving.

Flying wasn't the worst way to travel but he was definitely ready to be on the ground and away from the crowds.

He had packed light so only had a carry-on, which he hefted easily over his shoulder as he walked through the airport toward the exit. The canned Christmas music did a lot toward lightening his mood, especially when he heard Felicity's favorite song playing.

He'd been anxious about seeing Felicity again mostly because their text exchanges had been…well odd. Some of them intense and fun, others a little bit on the passionate side, still others were stilted. It was kind of par for course for their relationship. They both were juggling trying to be what the other wanted and still being true to themselves.

Lane paused inside the exit area, scanning the crowd for his brother but didn't see him. Fair enough since Hud did say that Emma had an OB appointment this morning so he might be running late. He started to pull his phone from his pocket when he caught a glimpse of a familiar figure in jeans, boots, a pink wool jacket and beanie, and his scarf.

Damn him, she looked good.

He stood there for a moment and just drank in the sight of her. He had missed a lot of people and places in his life and had experienced this feeling before. He recognized that keen sense of happiness that came from seeing a familiar face, but this was the first time it was a woman inspiring it. Not a family member.

"Hey," she said sort of shyly, waving at him. She shifted her purse from one shoulder to the other and then walked toward him. There were flakes of snow on her pink beanie and the top of her nose was red from the cold.

He waved back at her as she got closer and opened his arms, and she sort of hurried her last few steps and flung herself into his arms. Braced for it, he caught her easily and kept his balance. Holding her close, she smelled of the cold wind and snow but she felt like home. Warm, soft, welcoming.

Tears stung the back of his eyes and he thought he might be more tired than he realized. But he simply held her close for a long time.

"I missed you," she said. Lifting her head, she put her

gloved hands on his face and leaned up to kiss him, lightly on the lips. "I didn't think I would."

He felt the same. The intensity of his emotions for her surprised him. "Me too. Is everything okay with Hud and Emma?"

"Yes. I saw them yesterday morning at church and when Emma mentioned that she might have to go to her appointment alone…well, I hope you don't mind but I said I'd pick you up," she said, nibbling on her bottom lip and worrying off the lipstick that she had on.

"I don't mind. From the night I spent at your place, I'm with you," he said. He was starting to wonder if her ex might have cheated on her or if he had thought things were casual and Felicity hadn't. Lane wanted to know more about him so he could…well not make the same mistakes that guy had. Lane wanted Felicity in his life.

That had become crystal clear when he'd sat at a table for eight at the dinner and everyone else had a partner or spouse with him and the seat next to his had been empty. Before that hadn't mattered. He had his brothers—both the biological ones and the ones from the Corps—but now he wanted someone special.

Damn. That was sappy and he wasn't a sappy guy. But he didn't care. With Felicity…it felt right.

"Do you have any other luggage?" she asked.

"Nope. Just this," he said.

"Hudson mentioned that you'd probably need to walk

around a bit before just jumping in the car to drive back to Marietta. I hope you don't mind but I have an idea for something we could do," she said, leading him out of the airport toward the car park.

"What is it?"

"There is a Christmas tree exhibit at the MSU Arboretum and Botanical Gardens. They have it every year. They set it up in themes and I thought we could have lunch and check out the trees and then head back home."

"That sounds perfect to me," he said.

She drove the short way to MSU and parked her car. She talked a lot and he let her, just loving the sound of her voice. As she paused in front of the all-white exhibit he realized even the trees had been coated in something to make them sparkle. "I love this. When I was a little girl I thought that everything snowy and white was good. I was so disappointed when the White Witch in *The Lion, The Witch and The Wardrobe* turned out to be the baddie."

He threw his head back and laughed. The joy he felt was a little bit at her confession but a lot due to the fact that for all intents and purposes in this moment he felt like a regular guy. In Bozeman he didn't know as many people and to outsiders he knew that he and Felicity looked like a couple. He pulled her into his arms and took the kiss he'd wanted since he saw her waiting for him at the airport.

He put his hands on her butt, held her closer than some might deem appropriate, and showed her with his embrace just how much he'd missed her and how glad he was that she was here with him now.

⭐

FELICITY DROVE CAREFULLY back to Marietta. After that kiss…she felt like the changes she'd thought had been taking place between the two of them were real. That Lane did see her as more than just his Christmas girlfriend. It was a real thing; she knew from past experience that some men with big families needed a girlfriend for the holidays. Someone parents liked and the sisters-in-law approved of.

While she knew that Lane wasn't that type of guy, a part of her was still afraid to trust. Not just him, but also herself. It had been easy to fool herself before. And that was the cruelty of falling for someone. It was always headlong and felt so overwhelming and amazing and all she could do was hope that the guy felt the same.

She tried to glance at him surreptitiously from under her lashes but she noticed he was watching her.

"What are you thinking?" he asked. "You keep glancing my way and then turning your attention back to the road."

"I didn't think you'd notice," she said.

"Every time you take your eyes off the road the car drifts a little to the left and then you steer us back," he said.

She blushed. "I'm the worst for that. I have never been one of those drivers who can look at scenery and steer in a straight line."

"I'm scenery?" he asked.

"Well, I've made no secret of the fact that I like looking at you," she said. "I kind of have a muscly arm fetish and that shirt you are wearing…well it clings to your chests and biceps… It is a bit distracting."

He flexed his arms and sat up a bit straighter. "I had no idea."

She shrugged. "I'm not sure when it started but my obsession certainly wasn't abated when I saw Chris Evans as Captain America."

"Should I be jealous?" Lane asked.

"That I like guys with good looks and well-muscled arms who serve our country? No, I think you're good," she said with a small laugh. In a way Lane was everything that she'd ever pictured for herself. Of course her dream guy was always faceless—probably because she figured she'd know him when she saw him. She thought it fitting that her ex had never been the guy she saw in her dreams. Maybe it had been her subconscious telling her something.

"I'll make a note to keep working out," Lane said.

"You don't have to. I like other things about you too," she admitted.

"Like… Just kidding, I'm not fishing for compliments," he said.

"I know. That's one of the things. And you didn't freak out when I swerved while driving. I have the car under control even if I'm not a perfect driver," she said, realizing as she did so that she sounded defensive. She'd thought she'd gotten over defending herself but apparently she hadn't.

"It's okay. You should have seen me the first time I tried to drive with the prosthetics on. It took me a bit of time to get used to the pressure I needed to put on the gas."

"Did you have to get a special license?" she asked.

"No. Just had to prove I was roadworthy. Since I've retained a lot of control over my legs it was more me getting used to the prosthetics than anything else," Lane said.

"I can't imagine what that is like," she said. "I want to ask a million questions but they probably are all wildly inappropriate."

He shook his head. "Go on. My nephews asked me all kinds of things. And at first I was surprised then I realized that my brothers were hanging close and listening too. I think everyone wants to know something but isn't sure of the right way to say it. Ignoring it just makes me feel odd and probably doesn't make you too comfortable either," Lane said.

Leave it to Lane—a double amputee—to be so comfortable and at ease with himself that she felt silly not being relaxed about it.

"Well, when you walked around without the prosthetics at my place…how did you learn to do it? Is that normal?"

"It depends on the amount of damage. The way my legs are it isn't too bad for me to walk on the stumps," Lane said.

"Cool. I liked being taller than you," she said turning to

wink at him. The car drifted and she steered it back straight. "I'd never swerve off the road."

"I trust you, Felicity," he said.

"You do?"

"I do," he said. "Do you think you will ever trust me?"

She chewed her lower lip and deliberately didn't look at him. "What makes you think I "

"I'd rather you just say no than lie to me," he said.

She signaled and then steered the car onto the shoulder and put it in park before turning to face him. "I'm sorry. It's hard to admit that I don't trust as easily as I once did. But the truth is it's not you. I have a hard time depending on myself. My instincts aren't as great as I believed they were."

Lane took his seat belt off and turned more fully in the seat to face her. "Who hurt you?"

She swallowed hard. She hadn't meant to get into this. Not now. But really was there ever a good time to tell someone that you were an idiot? She didn't think so.

She sighed and closed her eyes. Remembering some of the things her ex had said to her. She felt stupid and odd. That she couldn't just act normal in this situation.

Lane put his hand on her shoulder. "It's okay. When you are ready to talk about it, I'm here. I'm not pushing you, but things…this is starting to feel real to me. I really did miss you, honey, and I want us to start building toward something more than just dating—"

"We've only been on one date," she said.

"I know. I want more," Lane said. "Which is why I brought up trust. Do you want more or is this just a fling?"

⭐

LANE KNEW THAT tiredness was playing into his candor. His legs hurt and he was just bushed from flying. He'd been up early and he wanted to be able to claim Felicity. He had realized earlier how important she was to him and he wanted to believe he meant as much to her, but he knew that in love sometimes both people weren't on the same place in the journey.

"Do you remember high school?" she asked. "I mean of course you remember but do you remember how one time we almost kissed?"

He nodded. He'd always been attracted to her. Felicity was one of those girls who had a smile for everyone and she had always just been so nice to him. Kind. And there had been that one moment in junior year when they'd both stayed after school for Spanish club and he'd leaned in close. She'd almost let him kiss her before she hugged him and grabbed her backpack and left the classroom. It had been…sobering. She'd made him feel like he'd read the signs wrong. He'd learned from that almost kiss.

"I do."

"Well, I wanted to kiss you so bad, Lane. You have no idea, but I thought I'd be bad at it and then I started worrying that you were doing it because you felt sorry for me and then—"

He put his finger over her mouth to stop her from talking. "That's crazy. A guy never kisses a girl because he feels sorry for her."

"Well, I didn't know that. I was so shy and scared and after I graduated from high school I decided to stop being scared. I figured what was the worst that could happen, right?"

He nodded.

"Well the worst is actually that you can think someone is a nice person and they turn out—"

"Who are we talking about here?" Lane asked.

"Johnny Bloom. Do you know him? He's from Cherry Lake," she said.

"I don't know him," Lane said. He wondered if his sister-in-law Lucy might since she had a lot of family in Cherry Lake.

"Well, he was cute—like you—and he's ranch bred—also like you. And we met at MSU when I was taking classes and we started dating and…over time it started to seem like I wasn't the person I thought I was. I mean I used to think I was nice and friendly, but Johnny said I was flirty. And I liked to cook but once we moved in together my food was dry or too spicy and—"

"Stop. I don't need to hear anything else to know that he wasn't a nice guy," Lane said. "Do you think I'm like him?"

"No. I don't or I wouldn't be here. But there is a part of

me that started to believe him, Lane. A part that thinks maybe I'm not nice and maybe I do think that things are more serious than they are. Not just with guys but also with women who were my friends. I just don't want to screw this up."

"How could you?"

She shrugged. "I don't trust myself. Sometimes…well, sometimes you make me forget everything and I'm just me. But I'm not sure of myself and I don't want to hurt you, Lane. You've always been special to me and you mean even more now. I just don't want to be the one to hurt you."

Lane understood that. He wasn't too eager to be hurt but he knew that no matter what Felicity decided he was already falling for her. Her honesty just drew him in even more. He didn't want to start something he couldn't finish on the side of the road but he knew that he wasn't going to easily let her go.

"I'm pretty resilient," he said at last. "And when I see something I want, Felicity Danvers, I don't just walk away."

"And you want me?"

"I think I've been pretty resolute about that," he admitted. "So are you going to take a chance on me?"

She bit her lower lip, not chewing on it but really biting it, and he saw the sheen of tears in her eyes in reaction to the bite. She nodded. "Yes. The entire time you were gone all I did was think about you. I couldn't sleep because I kept remembering you next to me and regretting that I didn't just roll over and cuddle close to you. I don't want any more regrets where you're concerned."

"Me either," he said. "No more regrets."

"I can't promise not to pull back again. Sometimes the way I feel about you scares me."

"Fair enough," he said. "As long as you don't lie to me we will be okay."

She nodded. "I made you something while you were gone."

"You did?"

"Yeah, it's in the green container in my bag," she said, reaching behind his seat and pulling out the container.

She handed it to him and he could see through the semi-transparent lid that there were cookies in there. Pinwheel cookies. He opened the lid and the scent of peppermint wafted up at him. The memory of his mom and all those happy Christmases rolled over him.

He closed his eyes as the nostalgia and loss roiled through him. He felt her hand on his thigh, squeezing, and then she reached over him and refastened his seat belt before putting the car in gear and driving again.

He didn't say a word—just ate the cookies she'd baked for him and knew deep in his gut that Felicity was definitely worth the pain that might come. She was special and he just had to figure out how to show her that.

Chapter Eleven

FELICITY PULLED INTO the driveway of Lane's house and turned off the car. He hadn't said anything else after she had handed him the cookies and frankly, she felt more vulnerable than she ever had before. He was probably tired from his trip and from going to the arboretum. It was getting dark because…well—winter. That's what happened this time of year.

She should drop him off and go home but she didn't want to. She wanted to stay with him and pretend they had already worked through all the stuff that was keeping them from being apart. Her fears, his…nothing. As usual Lane Scott was doing everything right. The man couldn't put a foot wrong even if it was a prosthetic foot he was placing.

He just rolled through life and kept coming up in the right spot, with the right attitude.

His Christmas lights came on, illuminating the front seat of her car, and she looked over at him.

"Want to come in?"

"Yes. But I know you might be tired and ready to be alone for a little while," she said.

He undid his seat belt and opened the door. "I'm actually tired of being by myself. I was alone in my hotel room each night, wishing you were with me. So what do you say we go inside and I heat us up a frozen pizza and we hang?"

"I'd love to," she said. She had even optimistically packed a change of clothes in her huge purse in case he asked her to stay over, so she'd be ready for school in the morning without having to go back to her place. She reached for her bag as he got out and retrieved his bag. She followed him up the steps into his house.

As soon as she stepped inside the scents peppermint and pine surrounded her. It was very Christmassy. He flicked on the hall light, which triggered his living room lights and his tree. She caught her breath as the multicolored tree was illuminated.

"You can hang your coat on the peg by the door," he said. "Boots can just sit underneath the peg."

"I have your scarf," she blurted out. "I found it at my place while you were gone. I bet you want it back."

"No. I like the thought of you wearing it," he said. "Keep it."

She smiled to herself as she took off her coat and boots and put everything where he'd asked her to. He took off his coat and then he led the way down the hall to the living room.

"I need to get changed and my prosthetics are chafing so I'll be a few minutes," Lane said.

"I'll fix dinner and get the fire going," she said. "Unless you need me."

"No. That will be perfect," he said.

He left the living room and she found her way into the kitchen. On the counter was a basket with muffins in it and a note from his brother Trey and his wife Lucy welcoming Lane home. She left that be and found the frozen pizza he'd mentioned and popped it in the oven. His fridge had a six-pack of beer, some old orange juice, and nothing else to drink. So she figured he might want beer.

She found the plates, which were not in the cabinets over the counter but in the ones below it. She figured that was so he could reach them in case he didn't want to use his prosthetics. She was coming to learn more about Lane and how he lived with his disability.

She lit a fire in the fireplace and surveyed the living room. The couch was large and made of leather. She ran her fingers along the supple lines of the cushions and then noticed there were a couple of pillows that were tucked against the back and into the side of the sofa. She left them where they were before going back to the kitchen.

She heard his footsteps and turned to see him standing in the doorway. He was wearing a pair of sweat pants that hung low on his hips and a thermal tee shirt that clung to his chest like a second skin. His hair was wet from a shower, she guessed, and she noticed that he'd left his prosthetics off. But it was the last thing she noted.

"Something smells good," he said.

"And it's almost ready to eat. Why don't you sit down and I'll get dinner for us?" she suggested.

"You don't have to wait on me," he said.

"I know. I just know how tired I am after a full day of travel and it's nice when someone else helps out," she said. It wasn't that she wanted to coddle him; it was just that it made her feel good to do something for him. To fix dinner…oh, no, she was doing it. Even though she wanted to be cool and let things unravel at a more natural pace, she couldn't help herself.

"Unless you don't want me to," she said after a few minutes of silence.

"Nah, I'm happy to let you do that. I recorded *The Santa Clause* while I was out of town. Want to watch it while we eat?"

"Sounds great," she said. "Oh, Trey and Lucy left you some muffins and a welcome home note in the kitchen."

"They have a key to my place and I suspect it's more Lucy's idea than Trey's, but they are always leaving me food on the counter."

"That's sweet," Felicity said, trying not to be envious of the closeness he shared with his family. Though to be fair she was close with her sister and mom too.

"It is, which is why I think it's Lucy's doing. Trey's just not that kind of guy."

"He's not? I don't really know him that well. I mean I've

heard of him and I know he still travels to do photography but I'm not really sure what else he does."

"Nothing special," Lane said with a wink. "He pales when compared to me."

Every man did. But she was smart enough not to say that out loud. Instead she fixed their plates and brought them to the living room with two beers and sat next to him watching the holiday movie with Tim Allen, trying not to feel like it was the perfect night. But she thought it definitely was.

☆

LANE CLEANED UP the dinner dishes and brought the container of peppermint pinwheel cookies back to the couch. He sat in his favorite spot and Felicity curled up next to him. He put the container of cookies on his lap and held her with one arm as they watched the end of the movie.

When he was asked in interviews the things he missed the most when he'd been deployed, he knew it was moments like this one. But they were too intimate to reveal in an interview—plus he hadn't had a steady girl in a while. But there was this sense of fulfillment deep inside of him as he held her. It wasn't about sex or need; it was about comfort.

Like he'd felt earlier at the airport. She was the one who made him feel content and he couldn't dismiss that. He thought about her past. How she'd dated a guy who made her feel so low and he felt tense.

She looked up at him and he realized he'd clenched his

hand into a fist, which had made his muscles flex. He tried to smile but he didn't want to brush it off that easily.

"Are you okay?" she asked.

"Yeah. I was just thinking about your ex and getting wound up about it," he admitted.

"It's okay. Don't let him bother you. A big part of it was that I was desperately wanting to be in a committed relationship…that's why I don't want to go too quickly with you," she admitted.

He got that but a part of him wanted to tell her that she was painting him with the same colors as her past if she did that. She had grown and changed and he was definitely a different guy than Johnny Bloom, whoever the hell he was.

"I read a quote while I was in Bethesda. It was one of those motivational posters that they have up all over the place at Walter Reed, and it said just because something bad happened doesn't mean you're on the wrong path. Sometimes the awful stuff is just the thing we need to point us toward the good stuff, you know?"

He didn't want to push her into something she wasn't ready for but he also had learned not to let things pass. That if he didn't talk to her about how he truly felt she might start thinking he didn't care. The way she had with the text message.

"You're right. It's just hard to take a leap off the same bridge."

"But the bridge is different," he said, sitting up a little

straighter. He debated for a second whether to go serious or light and there was something in her eyes—a wariness—that made the decision for him. "I mean I have these awesome pecs."

She arched her eyebrows at him. "You certainly do. Any chance I could convince you to take your shirt off?"

"Possibly."

"Good. What do I need to say? Please?" she said. Her voice was low and husky, brushing over his senses, arousing him.

He shifted on the sofa and she did as well, sitting back on her heels next to him, giving him room to take his shirt off. He took his time because he knew what he liked when he was looking at her. Slowly he tossed the shirt aside and when he turned she put her hand in the middle of his chest, urging him to sit so that his back was against the arm of the sofa.

She stood up next to the couch and he moved his legs so he was reclining. She slowly pulled her sweater up over her head and tossed it aside. She had on a thin thermal undershirt and no bra. He could see the pinkish red color of her nipples under the white fabric, which sent a jolt through his body. He shifted his legs to make room for his erection and she shimmied out of her jeans before climbing onto his lap.

"Wow. If I'd known what your reaction was going to be I would have taken my shirt off a long time ago," he said.

"I figured it was only fair for me to take my top off too,"

she said with a grin.

"I like the way you think," he said. But he liked a lot more than the way she thought. He put his hands on her waist and shifted her around until her center was rubbing over his shaft.

She had her hands on his chest, her fingers kneading the pads of his muscles. She ran her hands down his torso and then back up his arms, and he flexed them and heard her sigh.

"Wrap your legs around my waist," he ordered as he sat up and she did it. He shifted them on the couch and then turned so that she was under him. He put his hands on the arm above her head and did a push-up with her underneath him. She caught her breath.

"You are so beautiful," she said. "I love seeing you like this."

Her hands moved over his body. She traced the lines of his tattoo and then moved both of her hands up his arms, clutching at his biceps. She made him feel... well perfect. Like everything about him was exactly as it should be. He almost choked on the emotions that welled up inside of him.

That acceptance and her almost worship of this body. This broken body that he'd hated for a little while and resented some days still—even though he'd come to accept it. She loved it. She didn't see any flaws and that quiet acceptance made him want to show her that he accepted all of her.

His flaws were easier to deal with, he thought, because they were obvious and easy to see. Hers weren't. But that didn't make them any less important. He wanted to make this last but he needed more than he'd realized.

He reached between their bodies and freed himself from his pants and underwear. She lifted her hips so he could draw her panties down her legs. She parted her thighs and he slipped between them, felt the warmth of her center as he rubbed himself against her.

She arched her back, her breasts brushing against his chest. He lowered his head, tonguing her nipples through the fabric of her shirt and then suckling one into his mouth as he drew his hips back and found the opening in her body. He slipped inside of her and drove himself all the way home as she wrapped her legs around his waist and dug her heels into his back.

She clung to his arms, her fingers clutching at him while he braced one arm under her and then slipped one lower, lifting her hips and clutching at her buttocks as he drove into her again and again, driving them both higher.

He tore his mouth from her breast as he felt the first fingers of sensation down this back and he knew he was about to come, but he wanted to wait for her. He opened his eyes and groaned. Her head was tipped back, her mouth open on a moan and her eyes half closed.

He pulled back and plunged into her again, feeling his release start. He tried to stop it. He let go of her buttocks to reach between her legs and rub his finger over her clit until he felt her tightening around him as she called his name, and he let go. Thrusting into her again and again until he'd emptied himself inside her.

He collapsed against her, careful to keep his weight from crushing her, using his arms, but he rested his head against her breast. Felt her hands moving over his back, just languidly stroking him as if she couldn't get enough of touching him.

He knew then that he'd been wrong earlier when he'd thought he'd felt like he was home. Because this was truly home. In her body with her arms wrapped around him, he felt like he'd found something he'd been searching for far too long. The one thing he'd wanted but hadn't realized would be found here with Felicity and in Marietta of all places.

He'd searched all over the world for this even before his injury. He'd given up thinking he could find it after his injury and yet with Felicity here it was.

He hugged her close and rolled to his side. She was nestled against his side and his back was to the back of the couch. He held her close, not wanting to let her go, and she held him back just as fiercely.

He looked down at her and saw her watching him with those large light brown eyes of hers and he wanted to be worthy of the affection he saw there. Wanted to be the man who made all of her wishes come true at Christmas and throughout the rest of the year.

"Who knew that asking you to take off your shirt would have such consequences," she said with a tentative smile.

She was teasing again. Like he had done earlier. Both of them so wanting this to be okay. To not have any of the speed bumps they'd both experienced in relationships before. And he let her do it. Let her keep the mood light. But he had that tingling in his gut that warned something was coming.

It had to.

Nothing was ever going to be smooth all the time. If he'd ever believed that, he had quickly learned the truth while in the military.

"I had an idea it might," he said. "I'm glad it worked out the way it did."

"Did you have any doubts?"

"Not really. You make me hotter than a three-dollar pistol," he said.

She laughed and shook her head. "Where the heck did you hear that?"

"My dad. He says stuff like that all the time."

He knew he should get up and clean up and let her sit up, but he liked holding her and he hadn't had enough chances to do so before this. Just another few minutes and then he'd do it.

"What else does he say?"

"You can't catch moonlight," Lane said. Which always annoyed him growing up because he had thought his dad meant not to dream. "But I don't think that's true."

"Why not?" she asked.

"Because I've seen some of Trey's pictures of moonlight and I think he caught it."

But also because he refused to believe in impossibilities. Had left that behind on that street in Afghanistan and he wasn't going to pick it up again. And that—he decided—was what he needed to show Felicity. He needed her to believe it was possible to catch moonlight.

"I like that," she said.

He looked down at her and kissed her, slow and long, and when he lifted his head, he took a deep breath. "Wanna spend the night with me?"

"Yes. I packed a change of clothes in my bag in case you asked me," she admitted with that shy smile that made his heart beat a little bit faster.

He levered himself off the couch and she stood up beside him. Together they cleaned up the living room and went upstairs to his bedroom. They showered together, which was fun, and when he climbed into bed next to her, this time he didn't hesitate. He drew her into his arms, held her close to him, and got the best night's sleep he'd had in a long time.

Chapter Twelve

LANE WALKED THROUGH town toward the Graff Hotel. He was meeting his sisters-in-law Annie and Sienna and his nephews who were getting their annual pictures with Santa.

Lane had just come from a routine doctor's visit with Wyatt Gallagher to have an adjustment made on the sockets of his everyday prosthetics. Lane felt lucky that Wyatt had moved from Colorado back to Marietta. He was a top orthopedist and Lane had been seeing him since he'd returned. He had to have regular checkups to make sure that the prosthetics still fit and that his stumps were in good shape.

He stopped by the front desk of the hotel, checking to see if there was room available the night of the Christmas Ball. The event might have a different name but that was what all of his brothers had taken to calling it. They had sponsored a table at the event, which was being held to raise money for a local charity. Lane had been dreading a night sitting with his brothers and their wives but now he was looking forward to seeing Felicity all dressed up.

He had asked Felicity to be his date and she'd said yes. Now he wanted to make sure every detail was perfect. The Ball was this coming Saturday—a week before Christmas.

The Graff always straddled the line between modern luxury and the historical past of Marietta. The building was solid and decked out for the holidays in a very classy way. As he went to the front desk he paused to look at the grand staircase. He was looking forward to seeing Felicity on the stairs Saturday night. He wanted her to get ready here.

He booked a room just as his nephew Evan ran up to him. Hugging him and tousling his hair, Lane asked, "How was your day?"

"Good. We got the results back from our math test and I aced it. Mom helped me study and it paid off."

"I'm glad to hear it. I was always pretty bad at math," Lane admitted.

Evan slipped his hand into Lane's as they walked toward the main lobby where Santa was set up for photos. "That's okay, you're good at other things."

Lane smiled and shook his head. "Thanks."

"No problem. At home we believe in praising everyone," he said. "It doesn't matter if Dad burns dinner because he's good at running the tree farm. Stuff like that."

Lane liked the glimpse into this brother's home life that Evan afforded him. He also was proud of the lesson that Annie and Carson were teaching Evan. It was a valuable one.

"Not everyone is good at the same stuff," Lane said. Annie and Sienna were talking quietly when they got there and JT was frantically writing in his notebook.

"What is JT doing?"

"He is finishing up his homework," Sienna said. "I'm glad that Evan found you. We thought you might have forgotten."

"Never. I was running late. Did you all book rooms for Saturday night?" Lane asked.

"We did," Annie said.

"Alec is going to stay with me at my place here in town," Sienna added.

Lane didn't ask what the situation was but Alec and Sienna's marriage had been strained for a while. Sometimes they were together, like Saturday night, and then other times they both lived separately—Sienna in Marietta and Alec out on the Scott Ranch for weeks at a time.

"Sounds good. I just booked one and heard they are getting pretty full," Lane said.

"I think that's because there is some prince in town," Annie said. "Flo was telling me the latest while I was in there for coffee this afternoon."

"Done," JT said, tossing his notebook and pencil into his backpack.

"Yay," Lane said, to his nephew, getting a hug from JT. "So Santa photos?"

"Thanks for doing it with us, Uncle Lane," JT said. "Everyone at school said it was for babies until we told them you insisted on it."

"Well I like getting gifts at Christmas, so it makes sense I'd believe in Santa," Lane said.

"That's what Mom said. If you don't believe he won't bring you anything," JT said.

"I believe," Evan said.

"Me too," Lane said. "Let's get our photo."

There wasn't too much of a line to get the photo since most families came in during the Stroll to get their family photos. But there were a few families. Lane and his nephews had started the tradition two Christmases ago. The boys had been in that transitional stage and it had been important to Lane that he had something he did with his nephews. Something that was theirs.

The boys were really almost too big to sit on Santa's lap but they did it anyway while Lane stood to the left of the big guy. They all donned the red caps that Sienna had ordered for them, some kind of knit skullcap that was in the "ugly sweater" pattern.

After they finished with their photos they all headed over to the Main Street Diner as it was Wednesday night and the Scott men all had dinner together there. Sienna, Annie, Emma, and Lucy were going to have mani-pedis done while the men and boys ate chili.

Lane was often struck by how blessed he was to have this family and never more so on a Wednesday night when all of his brothers came to town and hung out together. Even when he'd been in the Corps if he could he'd video call so he could see them all.

The weekly meal together had started after Carson had lost his wife and Evan had been a baby. They'd all rallied together, showing the strength that came from their bond as brothers. They might not have had a clue about parenting but they'd all been there for Carson.

"Hi, Lane," Felicity said as she came out of the Mercantile. "What are you doing in town?"

"Just getting us a room for Saturday night," he said, waggling his eyebrows at her. They'd settled into dating and being very casual, keeping things light. One part of him really loved it because it suited the holiday season. But another part of him knew there were deeper issues that would have to be resolved if they were going to last past New Year's Eve.

"Good. I'm expecting the dress I ordered to arrive any day now," she said. "Just need to get my nails done and then I'll be ready."

"Want to join us tonight?" Annie asked. "The Scott men are all enjoying dinner at the Diner and us gals are having a salon night."

Felicity chewed her lower lip—something he knew she did when she was a bit nervous. "I'd love to. Do you mind if my sister joins us?"

"Not at all," Annie said. "The more the merrier. Lucy is bringing some wine a friend of her parents sent her from

California—so it should be fun."

"Great. What time?"

Lane waited to the side while the women discussed the details, but dropped a quick kiss on Felicity's cheek before she turned to leave with his sisters-in-law. As she walked away he realized that there was something settled and normal about his life. He wasn't faking it anymore.

☆

DRINKING HOT MULLED cider and sitting in front of the fireplace at the Graff with all of Lane's sisters-in-law was different. Her mom had stopped by and taken a photo of all of them before Andrea and she had left. Felicity enjoyed the other women's company and was very happy they included her, but she also was aware that she wasn't totally what they wanted her to be.

Lane and she were dating but both of them had been very careful since the night she'd picked him up at the airport. She wanted to pretend like her past was definitely behind her but every day she found herself changing in subtle little ways so that she could be what she thought Lane wanted in a woman.

She'd stopped wearing lipstick because his brother Trey had teased him when he noticed the faint stain on Lane's lips after he'd kissed her. She'd made him cookies again because he'd said how much he loved them—even though it was labor-intensive and it had meant she'd had to get up at four in the morning to finish grading papers. She'd…just been second-guessing everything and she knew it had to stop.

She wanted to be the woman she was. Not the woman she thought he wanted her to be, but it was hard. In her mind she still heard her ex's voice at times—saying things that she was better off ignoring, but it was hard to ignore. She wanted Lane to love her.

Damn.

Her hand shook as the realization sunk in.

"Are you okay?" Emma asked. She was seven months pregnant and glowing. She was also super sweet and had a southern drawl that made Felicity think of summer.

"Yes," Felicity said. "Just a little unsure if I should be here."

Emma reached over and patted her hand. "Girl, I know what you mean. These Scotts are overwhelming and then there are all of us now. It's hard to deal with falling for a guy and then have this overabundance of family to go with it. I'm just glad it was Gramps, Hudson, and me in the RV and not all of this. Made it easier to sort things out."

"You all are great."

"Of course we are," Annie said with a laugh. "Seriously, you fit in perfectly here. You have nothing to worry over."

If only it were that easy to allay her fears. But it wasn't. She had in her head how Lane's girlfriend should be and deep inside she felt…well she didn't know for sure.

"I think we need to go and get our men and let Lane and

Felicity have some time together," Sienna said.

"Oh, ho," Lucy said. "Are you and Alec patching things up?"

"We're always on the brink and then he does something else bullheaded and stubborn," Sienna said. "Honestly, I think he likes it when we fight."

"Only because you make up so well," Alec said, coming up with his brothers.

Sienna blushed and shook her head. She jumped to her feet to face her husband. "Where are the boys?"

"Your mom took them home with her. It's just you and me tonight, baby," Alec said wrapping Sienna in his arms and pulling her very close.

Felicity felt the heat of the embrace from where she was and turned away, realizing that Lane had done the same thing.

"Want to go look at the Christmas lights on Bramble Lane?" he asked, holding out his hand toward her.

She put her mulled cider on the table and got to her feet. "Thanks for inviting me along tonight, ladies."

Lane took her coat from her and held it up so she could push her arms into it. She wrapped his scarf around her neck before buttoning up her coat.

"You bet. I'm looking forward to seeing you both on Saturday night," Annie said.

The Scotts had purchased a table and they'd all be sitting together at the ball. She waved good-bye to everyone, noting that Alec and Sienna had already left as she and Lane exited the lobby and stepped out onto the street.

She pulled on her beanie and then took her gloves from her pocket as Lane pulled on his gloves. It was snowing again. Not heavily but enough to make the night seem almost magical.

On a night like this anything was possible, she thought. She took his hand in hers and then wrapped her arm around his and hugged him close. She was going to be herself. No more second-guessing. She wanted Lane in her life for a long time and she had to stop shooting herself in the foot emotionally by doubting everything she did.

"What was that for?"

"Just happy to have you here with me. This is the perfect Christmassy night," she said.

"Is it?" he asked. "We haven't even seen the first house. I think that it might be garish."

"I don't mind," she said. "That's one thing that my mom always seems to forget, but there is something tacky about Christmas that I love. I mean there are beautiful nativity sets and ornaments and I love a nicely themed house and tree, but there is something about a house that is decorated by someone who just loves Christmas so much they can't stick to one theme—that always gets to me."

"Me too," he said, stopping in front of the first house on Bramble Lane. A beautiful Victorian-style house that was tastefully decorated. Lane wrapped his arms around her and stood behind, resting his chin on her head as the snow fell around them. She felt for the first time that she might be enough for Lane. That she was more than good enough for him, and that warmed her heart and made her realize that she was starting to fall in love with him.

☆

"WHAT KIND OF house do you want?" Lane asked, as they reached the end of Bramble Lane and crossed the street to walk back up the other side. "I like my place but there are times when I wish I had more land. Monty and Risa live on a parcel of what used to be the Scott Ranch and I sort of envy them."

"I can see why you would," Felicity said. "I have always been a townie and not really a ranch person. I'm not sure I'd like being so far from everything."

"Fair enough. My place is out of the way compared to town," Lane said. "So is that too far?"

"No. It isn't. Since I teach it would be harder for me to be on a ranch," she said. "But if it's that important to you, I could do it."

There was a note in her voice: one that he was noticing more and more frequently that sounded like tension. It was whenever he said something and she tried to agree with him.

"Felicity, what are you doing?"

"What do you mean?"

"You don't have to change to please me," he said at last.

He hoped to hell he was wrong but that was what it felt like she was doing.

She hurried her pace. "I'm not doing that."

She dropped his hand and pulled her phone from her pocket, checking something on the screen. He struggled to keep up with her quickened pace. He was wearing his regular prosthetics and though he had them fitted with snow boots on the bottom, they weren't like his athletic prosthetics that enabled him to run. And he couldn't keep pace with her.

He stopped trying, walking at his own slower pace and waiting to see if she'd notice. Something was going on with Felicity, something more than he could figure out by just second-guessing her actions. He needed her to open up and talk about it.

Suddenly she stopped and turned to face him and he could see the sheen of tears in her eyes.

"Lane, I'm so sorry. But I think this isn't working," she said at last.

He caught up to her and lifted his gloved hand to wipe the tear from the corner of her eye. "Can we go back to your place and talk?"

"Yes. Let's do that," she said. "I am so thoughtless—walking too fast for you."

"It's okay to get mad or annoyed with me, Felicity. I know you're not going to always agree with everything I say. And, honey, I'm not always going to agree with you," he admitted.

"I know that. Truly I do but there is something inside of me that makes me… Let's talk when we get inside," she said. They had walked back over to Main Street and were almost at the alleyway that led to the back of Sweet Pea Flowers. She opened the door and led the way up the stairs to her loft apartment.

Once inside Lane headed for the kitchen table. Growing up, every serious conversation his family had ever taken part in was had around the table.

Felicity took off her coat and boots and Lane shrugged out of his coat, draping it over the back of the chair next to him. He didn't sit down, just rested his hands on the back of the chair and waited for Felicity.

"Do you want some hot chocolate?" she asked.

"Nah, I'm good. I'm more interested in hearing why you can't date me."

She wrapped her arms around her waist in one of the most defensive and protective poses he'd ever seen. It broke his heart. What had he done to make her feel this way?

"Felicity, honey, I'm not upset about anything you did," he started, trying to figure out how to reassure her.

She nodded. "It's not you. You're great, Lane. It's me. Every time I try to tell myself I'm just going to be me and stick to it, there is something inside of me that says it's not enough," Felicity said.

"That's not your voice," Lane said. "That's your ex. The truth is you are a wonderful woman and you don't have to change one damned thing for me."

She dropped her arms to her sides. "I know that. That's the worst part. I keep fighting against myself. I don't know what to do."

Lane walked over to her, his booted steps echoing in the quiet of her apartment. He stopped when they were only a few feet apart. "So when I first woke up in the hospital the only thing I could think about was what I'd lost."

"That's understandable," Felicity said.

"Thanks. But it's not very healthy. Remember I mentioned those posters at Walter Reed?"

"Yes, I do."

"Well I hated them. To me it seemed like all of those inspirational quotes were mocking me. It was easy for the doctors and nurses to be so positive, I thought. They weren't the ones dealing with the stuff I was," Lane said, taking a deep breath. "Then one day I get an email from Trey. He was shooting a story somewhere in the world and he had gotten one of those little quotes that are sometimes inside of juice bottles. The quote said: 'It's hard to defeat an enemy who has outposts in your head'. I don't know why that resonated with me when everything else didn't. But it struck me that I was defeating myself every day."

She nodded and in her eyes he knew she got what he was saying.

"So each day I started by saying to myself how much I loved my prosthetics," Lane said. "Just that. A few words that made all the difference in my attitude as I started using them and walking."

"I like that. But I don't know what I could say that would have that kind of impact on me," Felicity said.

Lane took a deep breath. He didn't like being vulnerable but he knew that one of them was going to have to lay their soul bare if they had any chance of making this relationship work. Something that Lane knew he needed.

"Just say Lane loves me just the way I am."

Chapter Thirteen

*L*ANE LOVES ME.

The words echoed in the stillness of the room and through her wounded heart. She didn't think or analyze, just hugged him close to her and kissed him. Not a sophisticated kiss, but one where her mouth was mashed against his.

She loved him too.

But she was afraid.

Fear should have no place in her mind or in her heart but it did.

"I guess you liked that," Lane said as she pulled away.

"I do very much…I love you too," she said.

"Good, right. That's settled then."

Settled? Not even close. But it did go a long way to relieving the feelings she had been battling with. She wasn't making this relationship into something it wasn't. Lane felt the same way.

"Right, honey?" he asked.

"Yes."

She could do this. She could fake it until she felt like she was in the right place. She'd done that for a long time when she first started teaching. Of course, no one had ever told her she wouldn't be a good teacher.

"That didn't sound believable at all," he said. "What is going on?"

"It's just that I'm afraid. There I said it. I'm afraid," she said. Admitting it actually made her feel a lot better. Like when she blurted things out. She hadn't done that lately because she'd been trying to be so good.

"We all have fear. I keep hoping I'm not rushing you and telling myself to slow down, but I can't," Lane said.

He took her hand in his and led her over the living room area and the sofa. He sat down and drew her down beside him. She noticed that he'd been walking more slowly and again was upset with herself for walking too fast earlier.

"How are your legs? Do they hurt? Do you want to take a bath?" she asked. "I ordered a new bath bomb and it came yesterday."

Lane smiled at her and if she had any doubts that he truly loved her they disappeared. The way he looked at her in that moment told her she was important to him and he cared deeply for her.

"I'm okay. I had the sockets adjusted today and I think I'm just not used to them yet," he said.

She was tempted to get distracted and then realized that was who she was. Her mind wasn't neatly organized and neither was she.

Lane loves me.

"Why did you have to have them adjusted?" she asked.

"My stumps sometimes change in size. In this case it might be because of the travel I just did, but I have to see my doctor to get the sockets adjusted," Lane explained. "Are you still afraid?"

"Yes," she admitted. But she realized that it didn't seem as insurmountable when she just relaxed and was true to herself. It seemed that when she tried to be what she thought Lane wanted—that was when she freaked out. "Are you?"

"Nope. Not anymore," he said, stretching his arm along the back of the couch.

"Why not?"

"Because you are here with me. You aren't running away or shoving me out the door," he said. "I think that means that you aren't as scared of us as you want to think you are."

She wasn't too sure she liked what he was saying but the truth was she did want Lane right here next to her. Her problems stemmed from things like seeing Johnny's new girlfriend at the salon and feeling inadequate again. Not for Johnny because he wasn't worth her energy, but for Lane.

"I saw my ex's new girlfriend tonight and she seemed so together—all the things I'm not. I guess it made me feel like even though I thought the problem was with Johnny maybe it was with me."

Lane shook his head. "I don't know the guy but I do know you, honey, and you don't have any problems. Well, that's not true. You try too hard to make things easier for everyone, not just me. And by doing that you wear yourself out. I don't think you have to try that hard."

She wanted to believe him. It would make life so much easier if she could just be like yeah, whatever, but that wasn't her. And Lane…Lane was so much more than she could ever be. She knew that. She owed it to him to at least be his equal in trying to make life better.

"Well, I just never measure up," she said at last. It wasn't just the problems with her ex, he'd just reiterated what she'd felt growing up. That she wasn't perfect, that she had too many flaws. And being in love with Lane made her realize that her flaws weren't as easily brushed aside as she'd like them to be.

"Stop it," he said at last. "You measure up just fine. Being in love with someone doesn't all of a sudden make you perfect."

"Not everyone feels that way," she said.

"Well I do. And there are only two people whose thoughts on this matter. You and me," he said.

"Agreed. What do you think makes a perfect couple?" she asked. Her throat was dry and her palms sweaty. He was asking for more than he realized and she was willing to give it to him because this was Lane. The boy she wished she'd kissed in high school. The boy who'd grown into a man she admired and called a hero. The man who had melted her heart and made her want to face her failings and flaws.

"I guess I'd say the perfect couple finds a way to smooth

out each other's rough edges. They take the good and the bad and blend them together into something solid that can't be broken. That's what I think we could have," Lane said. "If you'll give us a chance."

She nodded. She wanted that too. So much she was afraid. Dammit, when would she stop being scared?

"Will you give us that chance?"

⭐

LANE HADN'T ASKED for much in his life. Well, that was a slight exaggeration, he'd asked for a certain girl to like him in middle school, asked to make the football team, asked for his mom to live, and then much later when he'd been injured he'd asked to live.

He knew that sometimes gifts came into his life when he didn't get what he wanted the way he wanted it. In middle school that girl had turned out to be a lot prettier on the outside than on the inside, football had been hard and he hadn't loved it as much as he had thought he would. His mom—there would never be a time when he thought of her and didn't miss her, so he couldn't use that in this situation. But he had lived after the explosion and his life was much richer now than he'd thought it would ever be.

His future was tied to Felicity. He understood that he might be falling harder and faster for her than some people would say was sensible.

"Honey. Listen. Love isn't sensible; don't try to be rational about this. We fell for each other; don't try to deny it. There is nothing either of us can do to change that," Lane said.

"We could just walk away and ignore each other," Felicity said, but she didn't sound as if that was something she wanted to do.

He wondered if she wanted him to talk her into this. But then he felt his heart break a little bit. If he had to talk her into loving him then her emotions weren't real and wouldn't last.

"For the rest of our lives?" he asked a little angry.

"That would be dumb," Felicity said. "As would pretending that I am not going to give us a second chance. My hang-ups aren't about you or loving you. How could a woman not love you, Lane?"

Easily. He wanted to tell her about the other women in his life including the girlfriend who'd broken up with him just as he'd landed in Germany. Trey—his brother—had needed to relay the message to him. "I'm not perfect."

"You are to me. And that's why I worry. I want to be perfect to you, not this hot mess that you see before you."

He wanted to pull her into his arms but he knew if he did he'd want to make love to her—and if things got hot and heavy and physical they'd never finish this conversation. If he was coming to understand anything about Felicity it was that they needed to hash this out now.

"I'm the same underneath and, frankly, things have been

pretty good while we've started dating but there are times when I fail with the prosthetics or get angry about my legs and that's not attractive," he said.

She scooted closer to him on the couch and took his hand in hers, lifting it to her lips and kissing his knuckles. "I think that's perfectly justified. I get mad when I slip and fall on ice or when I lose my cool at school with a kid. I know better, I should be better, but I'm only human and so are you."

"That's what I've been trying to say to you. No one is going to always get it all right all the time," Lane said. "You have to take a risk."

"Risks scare me. I try to be brave a lot of the time but honestly I can't be. I don't want to be hurt or to hurt you. I know that might make me seem weak, but there it is."

"That's not weakness. Anyone who says otherwise is lying to you," Lane said. He knew that firsthand. He and Monty and his other Corps brothers had talked more than once about their experiences. Everyone always admitted to fear on one level or another. Even the most badass guys who on the outside seemed so cool under pressure were afraid of something.

"Okay." She nibbled her bottom lip as she watched him and he wasn't too sure what she waited for. What kind of reaction did she want from him? He was done guessing at her intentions; he needed her to spell it out.

"Okay?" he asked.

"Okay. Let's keep doing this," she said.

He shook his head and felt his heart start beating again—not the physical organ but his emotional center. It had stopped when he'd felt so close to losing her but now he was alive again.

He wanted to lift her into his arms and carry her to bed, but he couldn't. He really never would be able to and he regretted that. He grimaced and squeezed her hand tight in his.

"What is it?"

"I want to do the romantic thing and lift you up in my arms and carry you to bed," he admitted.

She made a tsking sound and stood up, pulling him to his feet next to her. "I don't need to be carried to bed, Lane. I just need you to hold my hand and go there with me. Loving me and being honest with me is the most romantic thing you can do."

He followed her across the loft to her bed and when they got there she pushed him down on the bed. They made love slowly, each kiss building to the next and each caress setting fire not only to his body but also to his soul.

And when he finally entered her he stopped and their eyes met.

"I love you," she said, wrapping her arms and legs around him and squeezing him tightly to her. "Don't ever give up on me."

"I love you too," he said, then started thrusting into her.

When they came together and he could catch his breath, he rolled to his side, holding her close to him. Just listening to her breath and seeing the Christmas lights in the living area he knew that he'd found the angel he'd always wished he could find.

★

FELICITY AND LANE had fallen into some very good patterns over the last three days. While she knew they were both in the honeymoon period of their relationship she felt much better about them as a couple. She had told Lane that she couldn't live on the ranch and didn't want to move from her loft apartment. She was happy there. It made her feel like she was living in the center of town.

Lane had agreed to living in town but he said the apartment wasn't the best choice for him, so he'd asked her to consider buying a house on Bramble Lane. Which she'd agreed to.

She'd taken to being honest with him about everything and she had been surprised how respectful Lane was of her opinions. But since he had always been so true to himself she wasn't that shocked.

Tonight was the big Christmas Ball and the dress she'd ordered was a formal floor-length ball gown. She didn't know what the Scott women were wearing. She didn't even know what her sister, Andrea, was wearing. Andrea was going with one of Lucy Scott's DeMarco cousins form

Cherry Lake.

She had a new confidence that had come from loving Lane and she was enjoying every second of it. She'd watched a YouTube video and fixed her hair in a very sophisticated up-do that mirrored one she'd seen an Oscar-winning actress wear on the night she'd won her award. And as she pirouetted in front of the mirror, Felicity thought she had done a pretty good job.

Her dress was made of a shimmering silver fabric at the top; it was strapless and fitted. The pattern on the bodice was swirling and then from the waist down it was draped silver tulle that fell to the floor. Her legs were almost visible through the tulle and she wore a choker necklace that she'd bought for herself when she'd graduated college. She didn't have any earrings in but that was only because she was still debating which pair to wear.

Lane was meeting her downstairs. He said he wanted to give her time to get ready and he wanted this night to be special for them.

There was a knock on the door and she took a minute to double-check her lipstick before she opened it.

"Felicity, oh, my God. You look gorgeous," Andrea said.

Her sister hugged her carefully. Andrea wore a red sheath dress in satin that left one shoulder bare, hugged her curves, and ended just above her knee. Her sister had left her straight hair down and had done a classic smoky eye for her makeup. Felicity felt a tinge of excitement seeing her sister all dressed up. There just weren't that many chances to do something like this in Marietta.

"You look gorgeous too. You know tonight I'm really happy we live here and that it's Christmas. I don't feel like we aren't living up to Mom's crazy perfect holiday expectations either."

"Ha! I think it's safe to say we are exceeding them. I'm not being a smartass, but I think being in love is giving you a glow," Andrea said. "I've never seen you look better. Lane is definitely the right guy for you."

Felicity agreed. "I never thought I'd be able to trust a guy enough to fall for someone again."

"Your ex was a douche. Speaking of which I heard he's in town for the ball. Just wanted to give you a heads-up."

Felicity didn't feel anything when she thought of Johnny being at the ball. Not like the day of the Stroll when the thought of running into him made her almost nauseous. Tonight she felt like a different woman. Heck, she was a different woman. She had claimed Lane Scott for her own and was taking her life back. One day at a time.

She and Andrea took a selfie. Felicity thought this was going to be the best Christmas ever. They got to the landing that led down to the main lobby and then to the ballroom and the grand staircase. Felicity noticed Lane waiting at the bottom with his brothers and Monty.

She heard the elevator open and turned to see the Scott wives coming down the hall. Emma Jean—the country music singer/songwriter who was almost eight months pregnant—glowed with an inner and outer beauty as she walked toward them. Her hair up but with a few tendrils to frame her heart-shaped face. Annie with her New York sophistication looked like she was on her way to a Met Gala, and Lucy the chef from California wore something simple and chic. On anyone else the dress would have seemed casual but not on Lucy. Risa looked like an ice queen but in the best way possible, but it was Sienna who stole the show. She was dressed like a woman who was ready to get her man back.

They all walked down the stairs together. Annie stopped them halfway.

"Ladies, we have the best-looking men in Marietta waiting for us," she said.

"We certainly do," Emma added. "But mine is the most handsome."

She went down the stairs to her waiting husband who pulled her into his arms and off her feet, kissing her as his brothers yee-hawed and claimed their own women. One by one the women all joined their men and walked into the ballroom. Soon it was just Lane waiting at the bottom for her.

Felicity took the steps slowly because she didn't want to trip and because she couldn't take her eyes off Lane in his formal wear. His tux had to be custom-made; it fit him to perfection. His hair had been slicked back and his jaw—

always strong—had been close shaven.

When she reached the bottom step he came forward and wrapped his arm around her waist, lifting her slightly. She wrapped her arms around his shoulders and kissed him deeply. Knowing she'd found the one man she'd been searching for right here where she'd least expected him.

"I think this is going to be beginning of a very beautiful life," Lane said.

She just started laughing and then kissed him. "I love you, Lane Scott."

Epilogue

LANE HAD A busy January and had been to DC twice—once to speak to a group of veterans and the other time to testify in front of a house subcommittee. He was back in Marietta just before Valentine's Day and just in time to surprise Felicity at school. He waited in the parking lot away from the car pick-up line until her last student had been collected, and then he pulled up in front of the school and waved at her.

She came over to the car and he put down his passenger window. "You're back early."

"I wanted to surprise you," he said. "Can you leave now?"

"Yes. I just need to grab my bag."

"I'll wait," he said.

He'd been planning this since New Year's Eve when they'd attended the masquerade at the Graff. When they'd kissed at midnight he knew he wanted to ask her to be his wife, but he also wanted to give them a little more time together. Let them live their normal lives and see how they melded.

It hadn't been easy for him to wait because he wanted her to be his wife. But he'd hoped she'd feel more confident if he waited. This was the day though. Valentine's seemed like a good time to propose and the realtor had called him this morning and told him he could pick up the keys to the house they'd purchased on Bramble Lane.

He wanted to start their lives together there.

She came back out and his breath caught as she smiled at him. She made him feel like he was the hero everyone always said he was. She made him feel alive in a way that nothing else had. As soon as she climbed into the cab of the truck he leaned over and kissed her. It was long and deep and too hot for an embrace outside of a school.

He pulled back and noticed her skin was flushed. "I hope you are taking me home so I can show you how much I missed you."

"I am," he said. "But we need to make a stop first."

He drove through town to Bramble Lane and then up the street to the house that had a sold sign in front of it. He parked in the driveway and came around to open her door.

Felicity hopped out. "I can't wait until this place is ours."

He held up the keys. "It is."

"This day keeps getting better and better," she said.

They joined hands together and walked up to the house. He'd asked the realtor to have the heat turned on in the house for them and when they opened the door it was toasty and warm. She started to take a step forward but he stopped her.

He'd been practicing at the gym with Monty and Hudson who were a lot bigger than Felicity, but they were the only ones he'd had to practice with. He wanted to be able to lift her and take one step over the threshold. Before he'd left for DC this last time he'd finally been able to do it with his brother.

"What?"

"I want to carry you over the threshold," he said.

"It's okay. I know you can't."

"Do you?" he asked, lifting her into his arms. She was very still at first. "Put your arms around my shoulders."

She did and he stood there for a minute, getting his balance with her weight, and then took a deep breath and took one step and then another. As soon as they were over the threshold, he carefully lowered her to her feet.

She hugged him so tightly that he knew his work was well worth it. "I love you. Thank you for doing that."

"Well it's only fitting that a man carry his woman into the house they are going to build their life together in," he said.

She nodded. "It is."

He fumbled in his pocket, pulling out the small jeweler's box. He'd picked the ring up when he'd been in DC.

"Lane…"

"Felicity," he said. "From the moment you crashed into me on Main Street I knew my life was going to change. You made me feel alive—something that I hadn't felt in a long time. I'd just existed and was sort of seeking some new path, but I didn't think it would be this one. You've surprised me at every turn, made me fall in love with you, and given the kind of happiness that I thought my brothers were making up before I experienced it with you.

"I'd go down on one knee but I can't manage that. You are my life, my soul, my everything. Will you marry me?"

"Yes! A hundred times yes. You are the man of my dreams, Lane Scott. I can't imagine spending a day without you by my side. You make me feel like I'm perfect even with my flaws. I love you so much."

He slipped the ring on her finger and pulled her into his arms, kissing her slowly and deeply.

Someone cleared their throat and Lane broke the kiss, looking over his shoulder to see all of his brothers, sisters-in-law, and nephews standing there alongside Felicity's mom and her sister, Andrea. He'd invited them over because engagements were meant to be shared with family.

"I guess she said yes," Carson said.

"Of course I did," Felicity said.

"Welcome to the family," Alec said as the family filed into Felicity and Lane's new home. Lane realized he'd found something he'd been searching for right where he least expected it.

The End

More by Katherine Garbera

THE SCOTT BROTHERS

Book 1: *A Cowboy for Christmas*
Carson Scott's story

Book 2: *The Cowboy's Reluctant Bride*
Monty Davison's story

Book 3: *Her Summer Cowboy*
Hudson Scott's story

Book 4: *Cowboy, It's Cold Outside*
Trey Scott's story

Book 5: *Her Christmas Cowboy*
Lane Scott's story
Leave a review!

Available now at your favorite online retailer!

ABOUT THE AUTHOR

USA Today bestselling author **Katherine Garbera** is a two-time Maggie winner who has written more than 60 books. A Florida native who grew up to travel the globe, Katherine now makes her home in the Midlands of the UK with her husband, two children and a very spoiled miniature dachshund.

For more from Katherine, visit KatherineGarbera.com

Thank you for reading

Her Christmas Cowboy

If you enjoyed this book, you can find more from all our great authors at TulePublishing.com, or from your favorite online retailer.

Printed in Great Britain
by Amazon